George Bryce

John Black - the Apostle of the Red River

How the blue banner was unfurled on Manitoba prairies

George Bryce

John Black - the Apostle of the Red River
How the blue banner was unfurled on Manitoba prairies

ISBN/EAN: 9783337302399

Printed in Europe, USA, Canada, Australia, Japan

Cover: Foto ©Andreas Hilbeck / pixelio.de

More available books at **www.hansebooks.com**

JOHN BLACK

THE APOSTLE OF THE RED RIVER

OR,

HOW THE BLUE BANNER WAS UNFURLED ON MANITOBA PRAIRIES

BY

REV. GEORGE BRYCE, M.A., LL.D.

Professor in Manitoba College, Winnipeg.

TORONTO:

WILLIAM BRIGGS

WESLEY BUILDINGS.

C. W. COATES, MONTREAL.   S. F. HUESTIS, HALIFAX.

1898

PREFACE.

WE are in the habit of referring to the heroic deeds of our fathers, whether English, Scottish, Irish or French, in the struggles they endured and the sacrifices they made for country or religion. The service rendered to liberty and religion by Cromwell and his Ironsides at Marston Moor or Naseby, by Hamilton and his Covenanters at Drumclog, by King William and his followers at Boyne and London-derry, or by Henry and his Huguenots at Ivry, may well stir our bosoms with emotion.

But this century has, in the piping times of peace, devel-oped a new and, perhaps, greater heroism in the army of Christian adventurers going to all lands, and proclaiming under King Jesus a war against sin and idolatry, in which battles for the truth are fought against "principalities and powers" as real as those against Prince Rupert, or the bloody Claverhouse. Even the quieter life of a pioneer missionary like Carey or Livingstone requires the highest daring and the sublimest perseverance.

To this class belongs the career of Rev. John Black, the Apostle of the Red River of the North. To leave home and friends at the call of duty, to cross the trackless prairies of the north-western States in order to reach the northern and secluded plains of Rupert's Land, to bury himself in obscurity, albeit he was engaged in laying the foundation of a spiritual empire of the future, was to give John Black a true claim to the honor of self-sacrificing fame and highest patriotism.

The work of the author has been a labor of love, and it is with the hope of awakening wider interest—especially in the minds of the young—in the sweetness of self-sacrifice, and in what the world may call the "reproach of the cross," that this little book is sent forth.

CONTENTS.

ILLUSTRATIONS.

JOHN BLACK

THE APOSTLE OF THE RED RIVER

CHAPTER I.

His Early Days.

John Black was the Apostle of the Red River. He will be long remembered on the prairies of Manitoba. In 1882 he passed away, all too soon to see the remarkable rise of the country for which he had planned and worked and prayed. He had reached the age of sixty-two, and nearly half of that time he had spent on the plains of the Northwest. His name is a household word in many settlements, and his memory is revered by the white settlers and the Christian red men alike, throughout Manitoba, Saskatchewan, and Alberta.

BIRTHPLACE AND CHILDHOOD.

On a visit to Scotland, a few years ago, the writer of these sketches spent a few pleasant days on the Scottish border. He was guest of a former Canadian minister in the pretty parish on the river Esk, of which Sir Walter Scott speaks, where "there was racing and chasing on Cannobie Lee." One day a delightful drive led along the winding valley of the river to the town of Langholm, to attend the Presbytery meeting there. After the business was over the Presbytery dinner was held, with all the forms of the "olden time." While at dinner one of the ministers addressed the writer : " Oh, I'm the minister of Eskdale Muir, where your first minister on the Red River, the Rev. John Black, was born." It was interesting to note that the pioneer of the western wilds was not forgotten in the place of his birth.

On the 8th of January, 1818, John Black was born. He was the son of William Black and Margaret Halliday, Eskdale shepherd farmers, who lived on the farm of Garwaldshiels. His ancestors had originally dwelt in the neighboring parish of Ettrick, and some of them had been warm friends of the godly minister there, Thomas Boston, whose works, " Fourfold State " and the " Crook in the Lot," were well-read books in many a Scottish home.

The farm of Garwaldshiels was a lonely spot. Its steading, as the farm buildings are called in Scotland, was two miles from any other. Indeed, the whole parish of Eskdale Muir is mountainous and sparsely settled, its inhabitants being chiefly sheep farmers and shepherds. In the church on Sunday it is said the collie dogs were formerly almost as many as the men. Sometimes the dogs became restless, and were apt to disturb the minister.

The shepherds of the south of Scotland are noted as a most intelligent lot of men. Their quiet life on the hills with their flocks gives them time for thought. They are great readers, and undertake to master the deepest books. This is so uncommon among humble people, such as they, that visitors from outside Scotland are greatly struck by it. It is said that a Yorkshire wool merchant once visited the parish of Eskdale Muir on business, and was so surprised that he said : " They are the strangest people that ever I saw ; the very shepherds talk about deep stoof (stuff)."

The minister of this parish who baptized John Black was in knowledge a leader of his people, for he was the author of a work called " Antiquities of the Jews," which was for-merly very well known.

About the time of the birth of John Black, the shep-herds of the border parishes had gained another accom-plishment. Many of them undertook to write poems. The reason of this was that a few years before, in the parish of Ettrick, a remarkable man, James Hogg, known as the " Ettrick Shepherd," had written a number of very beauti-ful poems, which had been published and widely read. This led many of the shepherds to imitate one of their own number. Some of the poems produced were poor, but others were uncommonly good. It was strange to see such a burst of song in a people so severe in their thought.

Born of such a stock, and brought up in such surround-ings, it was no wonder that the boy of Eskdale Muir should early show a disposition to study. He had a great thirst for knowledge, even as a child, and especially for Bible stories and religious thoughts. In early childhood, we are told, he was noted for his affectionate disposition. He was a serious boy, and even early in life, at the age when most children are thoughtless and unconcerned, he showed a desire to become a follower of Jesus Christ.

REMOVAL TO HIGHMOOR.

When John Black was a boy of seven years of age his family removed from the lonely farm of Garwaldshiels to Highmoor, some twenty miles to the south. Highmoor was situated in the parish of Kilpatrick-Fleming. It was a sheep farm, of about 700 acres, and belonged to a cele-brated border family, the Maxwells of Springkeld. It was in the very centre of historic ground. It was less than five miles from the Scottish border where the little stream-let that divides Scotland from England marks the change from the broad Doric tongue to the very different dialect of Cumberland. From the door of Highmoor the Solway Frith was clearly in view, with its small sailing vessels and greater ships passing on the errands of commerce.

Between Highmoor farm and the Solway was not more than ten miles, and a beautiful little stream, the " Kirtle Water," ran through the farm and emptied into the frith. The windings and turns of the " Kirtle " are well filled with the thoughts of romance, and within this short dis-tance seven old castles are to be seen, the strongholds of the Irvings and the Bells, so well known along the Scottish border. These old castles all had their legends, and almost every one of them was said by country folk to have been the scene of some great crime, and to be haunted by a ghost or evil spirit. While John Black did not believe these old tales, he was always fond of the stories, and read with greatest interest the " Tales of the Border," and Sir Walter Scott's poems of the border minstrelsy.

Highmoor was not more than four miles from Eccle-fechan, the town where the great Scottish writer, Thomas Carlyle, was born. Not half that distance from Highmoor was the house where Carlyle's father, mother, and brother long lived. Even the Hodden Hill farm, which Thomas Carlyle for a time occupied, was not far from Highmoor. Upon this farm was a celebrated erection known as the "Tower of Repentance." On this farm Carlyle was just becoming known as a genius in the days of John Black's boy-hood, and what were called his " longnebbit " words and striking sayings were often spoken of by his Annandale neighbors. John Black, to the day of his death, was proud of his fellow-dalesman, who became known as the "Sage of Chelsea."

The wider view from Highmoor was equally beautiful. Looking eastward to the end of the Solway Frith, one could see the tall chimneys of the city of Carlisle, so prominent a place in the border strife. Towering to the sky were to be seen beyond in Cumberland the gigantic Skiddaw and other mountains, while beyond the heights of Cumberland appeared dimly the Yorkshire fells and the hills of Durham. To the west the far view was interesting. Majestic Criffel appeared running out into the frith, and on a clear day the hills of the Isle of Man were seen in the middle of the Irish Sea. Such a country, with natural beauty and historic memories, could scarcely fail to inspire those who dwelt in it. We are not surprised that John Black was stirred to poetry in such surroundings, and we learn that, following the beginning as a verse-writer, made under the name of "Glenkirtle" in the newspaper of his county, he all his life had a faculty of writing snatches of lively verse for his children and friends.

SCHOOLS AND SCHOOLMASTERS.

The parish school in the wide parish of Kilpatrick-Fleming was seven miles from Highmoor, but a second school, known as the "Gair school," was at the corner of the farm. Here, in 1826, John Black and one of his sisters began their education. The school was under the charge of a Mr. William Smith, the father of one afterwards well known in the Presbyterian Church in Canada, the Rev. Dr. Thomas Smith, at one time minister in Kingston, Ontario. To this school came from far and near pupils from the scattered farms, some of them boarding in the nearest dwellings. The parish schools of Scotland taught everything from the alphabet to the works of the highest Latin and Greek writers. Mr. Smith was a good scholar and a good teacher. Young John Black here laid a good foundation for his future attainments. Mr. Smith was followed as a teacher by Mr. John Roddick, also a man of much ability and skill as a teacher. He was, strange to say, the father of another Canadian, Dr. Richard Roddick, of Montreal. Under Mr. Roddick John Black made remarkable progress. The young scholar had a great fondness for the languages. The sturdy lad had, however, to fight with obstacles in getting an education. To make a living on the farm his father needed the help of all his children, and John could not well be spared when he had reached the age when he could herd the cattle and watch the sheep. He was often unable to be present at school, but his desire to gain a higher education never left him. At last his father consented to his study of the languages, and the happy boy at the age of fifteen threw all his energy into his task.

French was the first language on which he began under Mr. Roddick. A curious incident is connected with his entrance on the study of French. Full of the thought of beginning a foreign language he walked all the way to the town of Annan, nine miles distant, to buy a French grammar. On arriving in the town, he found the bookseller's shop shut and the bookseller along with almost all the people in the town, wending their way, week-day though it was, to the parish church. The boy followed the crowd, and found the greatest excitement prevailing. It was the day of the trial of the celebrated Edward Irving. Irving

was a native of Annan and a great friend of Thomas
Carlyle. He was a minister of great eloquence, who had
first assisted Dr. Chalmers in Glasgow, and afterwards been
settled in London. He had adopted strange views as to
the humanity of Christ, and on the day of John Black's
visit was being tried for heresy by the Presbytery of Annan.
The boy was present during the whole trial, and was wont
to tell to his latest day of the prophet-like Irving as he
answered for himself and of Dr. Henry Duncan, who was
the advocate for a pure doctrine and a divine Christ.
Thomas Carlyle in his " Reminiscences," defends his friend
and throws ridicule on the Presbytery, but the extravagant
views of Irving, remarkable man though he was, justified,
to the mind of most of the people, the action that was
taken by the Presbytery in deposing him from the sacred
office of the ministry.

The young scholar was able after the exciting scenes of
the day to find his way into the bookseller's shop, bought
the French grammar, and returned home to begin his study
with much enthusiasm. It was always his view that this
French grammar exercised a great influence on his after life.
It was through his knowledge of French that he was afterwards chosen, as we shall see, to work among the French-
Canadians, and it was thus through his being unattached
to any special congregation that he was led to find his way
to Red River.

The young scholar progressed very rapidly in his studies.
Of Latin and Greek he was very fond, while his love for the
great authors of his own language was intense. He had a
great craving for books. At the time of which we write,
and in a country district in Scotland, books were not easy
to be had. Fortunately for the young bookworm, a

" Library Association " was formed in the village of Water-back, which lay one mile to the west of Highmoor. Though the number of works was small, yet it represented nearly all classes of books. Twenty huge volumes of Brewster's Edinburgh Encyclopædia were there, and it is believed that John Black before the age of twenty had pretty well read them through. As a shareholder of the association, he made full use of his privileges. He read widely in history, both ecclesiastical and general, and made a brave attempt to grapple with the thought of such writers as Bacon, Locke, Butler, and Paley.

During this time also his religious life became stronger and more devoted. The parish minister was Rev. George Hastie, an earnest and devoted preacher of the Gospel. Under Mr. Hastie's instruction, and watered by the dew of heaven, the seed of truth, planted in early childhood, sprouted and grew into a flourishing plant. The young student made, under the faithful pastor, a public profession of his faith in Christ. He was also much strengthened in the faith by his youthful companions of kindred Christian feelings. One of these, Walter Smith, became afterwards Free Church minister of Half-Morton in Eskdale. Many years after, in a letter written from Red River to his brother, we find John Black speaking of this Christian friend in far-off Eskdale.

At about the age of twenty, his old teacher, Mr. Roddick, having left Gair school to accept a position in Liverpool, John Black was, for a time, called on to act as a substitute. This he did with much satisfaction to parents and pupils. It may have been this temporary work that suggested to the young man, who was rather retiring and bashful, the thought of teaching elsewhere. For some time after this he was engaged in teaching a school in one of the most beautiful and romantic villages of Cumberland. While gaining great success in his school in England, his mind was dwelling on the fuller devotion of himself to the higher office of the ministry. The ministry had thus early a great attraction to him. He, however, hesitated, for there was, to the end of his life, a singular union of courage and diffidence in Mr. Black. It was his disposition never to push himself forward in any cause, but if it seemed to him a duty he would go through fire and through water to accomplish it.

TO AMERICA.

He had now reached the age of twenty-three, when a complete overturn took place in all his plans. From hints thrown out in after years it is made plain that his father's family had not been prosperous in their sixteen years at Highmoor farm. It seems that they were so severely tried that they were compelled to borrow money to take them to a new land. John Black was his father's chief stay and counsellor, and so, giving up all the prospects in his English school, he threw in his lot with the rest of his family, and determined to go with them to America.

It was a sad picture when the family was torn up by the roots from the home where it had grown. The far-off Solway was to be left behind, the gently flowing Kirtle to be deserted, school and church, where character has been formed, to be forsaken, and the sweet glens and historic rivers and market town were to be seen no more. Oh, how sad the spectacle so often witnessed at the Broomielaw in Glasgow or on the docks of Liverpool, where tens of thousands have thus been wrenched from the tender associations of home, and thrust out into the wide world ! On June 18th, 1841, John Black, with father and mother, three brothers and four sisters, formed one of these sad companies, and, none too well provided with worldly goods, started from Liverpool to gain a living in the New World.

CHAPTER II.

Student and Missionary.

It was, as has been said, in the summer of 1841, that John Black's father with his family arrived in America. Though Canada was at this time enjoying a large British immigration, yet the family of Highmoor was led to find its way to the United States. Two sisters of William Black, with their husbands, had years before found a comfortable home in the State of New York. Twenty years' residence had made these Murray and Davidson families fairly prosperous, and to their rocky home the immigrants from Scotland came, ascending the Hudson River, reaching Catskill, and then going by land carriage to Bovina, in the county of Delaware. This region of the Catskill Mountains, though not suited for ordinary agriculture, has long enjoyed, from its sweet grasses and clear streams, a great pre-eminence as a dairy-farming district. No doubt this was due to the skill, energy, and thrift of the farmers from the south of Scotland who had settled there.

After reaching Bovina, the newly-arrived family took a farm in the neighborhood. For a time John gave some help in the work, but his heart was set on preaching the
2

Gospel. In order to obtain the means of continuing his studies, he engaged in teaching, and by his skill and enthusiasm awakened much interest in education among the young people of Bovina. The work of teaching John Black found to be an excellent preparation for the work of the ministry. The power to manage a school, the ability to understand the character of his scholars, and the habit of patience acquired were to him of great value in after life.

Desiring to carry on his education further before entering on the special study for the ministry, the young teacher looked about for an academy where he might pursue his general studies. This he found in Delhi, the chief town of Delaware county. Here a most accomplished teacher, Rev. Daniel Shepherd, was in charge of a school of a very high order. It is said that though this institution did not bear the name of either college or university, and gave no degrees, yet in scholarship many of its alumni were not behind university graduates.

John Black, now on fire with a high purpose, threw himself with all his soul into his studies. He at once took a high place in the school. The shepherd lad from the Gair school in far-off Eskdale reflected credit on his old teacher, Mr. Roddick. He planned a course of study in the needful branches of mathematics, but his chief delight was in classics. So excellent a scholar was he in Greek that the original Greek oration delivered by him on leaving the institution was for many years spoken of as being unusually meritorious. His metrical translations of Latin authors, such as Horace, were well done, and though not so often as formerly, yet now and then his muse took a poetic flight.

Like many Scottish students, John Black lived very economically in his school life in Delhi, "cultivating," as has been said, "the muses on a little oatmeal." With him were two of his cousins as room-mates, William and David Murray. These three lads, living in a little upstairs room, cooking for themselves the provisions received from home, gained in after life, though in different spheres, high and honorable distinction. William Murray became Judge of the Supreme Court of New York, and Dr. David Murray was the organizer of the educational system of Japan, and for several years chief superintendent of education there. When he left Japan to return to America he was invested by the Emperor with the highest order of Japanese nobility. He has since been State Librarian at Albany, New York. John Black may not have received such earthly honors as fell to the lot of his cousins, although he had his share of these, too, but he has the joy of those of whom it is said "they shall shine as the stars for ever and ever."

CHURCH LIFE.

Though baptized in the Church of Scotland, and attached to its forms, John Black became, on his arrival in Bovina, an active member of the "Associate Church." This was one of the bodies which afterwards were united and became the "United Presbyterian Church of North America." The minister of the Bovina congregation was Rev. John Graham, a native of Montrose, Scotland, a man of ability, especially as a writer. Before his death he published his "Autobiography," a most interesting book. Of Mr. Graham it was said that he "was a man with eccentricities, but far more excellencies." In Mr. Graham John Black found a true friend, as he did also in

the other members of the congregation. True piety prevailed among them. Perhaps some would call them nar-
row, but they were genuine. They had brought with them
from the old land customs such as the regular observance
of family worship, the keeping of the Sabbath, and the
habit of churchgoing, and these they put into practice in
their new world home. As the country settled, many congregations, which are now strong, hived off from the original one in Bovina.

For three years John Black remained a member of this
congregation, and his family were very anxious that he
should study for the ministry in connection with the
Associate Church. He was unable to accept all the
views of the Church, however, and this kept him for some
time in grave doubt. The Associate Church held that the
Scottish covenants were binding on the Church in later
times. It will be remembered that these covenants of
1638 and 1643 represent one of the grandest periods in
Scottish history. Nobles and people alike, in Greyfriars
churchyard, Edinburgh, and elsewhere in Scotland, signed,
in some cases with pens dipped in their own blood, the
covenant or pledge to oppose prelacy and popery, and to
keep the Church of Scotland pure and true. John Black
loved and admired the martyrs and Covenanters who fought
so nobly for liberty, but he was not sure that two centuries
after those stirring times it was still necessary to subscribe
these notable documents. The Associate Church required
of those who entered its ministry to declare adhesion to
"public covenanting," and this threw an obstacle in the
way of the young candidate.

His thought was then turned to Princeton College, the
seminary of the Old School Presbyterian Church, as it was

then called. Some five or six years before this time the Presbyterian Church of the United States had been rent by doctrinal differences, and perhaps more especially by the question of negro slavery. Princeton College would have satisfied the young aspirant to the ministry, but belonging, as it did, to the body which seemed unsound on the slavery question, John Black, like all of British blood, was horrified at the thought of being connected in any way with so hideous and cruel a thing as slavery, and so he could not conscientiously join the Old School. He still kept up correspondence with Scotland, and his love was strong for the Scottish Church. At this time, too, a great religious movement was going on in Scotland, which led to the Disruption in 1843, and the formation of the Free Church of Scotland. After this event the young student in Bovina began to turn his attention to Canada, where the Church was strongly Scottish in its character and customs.

Just at this time, early in 1844, a minister from Canada came on a visit to his friends in Bovina. This was the Rev. James George, then a minister of the Church of Scotland in Scarboro, in Upper Canada. Mr. George's father and brothers were nearest neighbors of William Black and his family in Bovina. Mr. George was at this time an examiner in Queen's College, Kingston, and, indeed, afterwards became a professor in that institution. Young John Black called upon Mr. George during his visit to Bovina, and enquired as to the opportunities for studying for the ministry in the Canadian Church. He also sought information as to what the Church in Canada would do in view of the disruption which had taken place in the mother Church in Scotland. Mr. George stated that he had a strong hope that the Church in Canada would satisfy all parties, and thus prevent a division on this side of the Atlantic. Having examined Mr. Black, Mr. George expressed himself as highly satisfied, and advised the young student to come over to Canada in the autumn and to enter Queen's College. Mr. George returned to Canada, the Canadian Synod met shortly afterwards in Kingston, and there the disruption took place. Mr. George thereupon wrote to Mr. Black informing him as to what had happened, but still urging him to come over and enter Queen's College on its opening. After all the kindness which had been shown him he felt it to be a painful trial to refuse ; but John Black's sympathies were with the Free Church in the struggle, and he could not accept the kind invitation of his friend. It was with great grief that he saw the division in Canadian Presbyterianism. He never ceased to desire reconciliation, and he was greatly overjoyed that he lived to see the happy reunion in 1875.

COLLEGE LIFE.

John Black had not an acquaintance in Canada other than Mr. George. He had noticed in the newspapers that the Rev. Mark Y. Stark, of Dundas, had been moderator of the synod at the time of its division, and that he had taken the side with which he himself sympathized. Accordingly, he wrote to this gentleman about the arrangements for starting a college in connection with the new body, and the answer came, greatly to his satisfaction, that the commission of synod would meet in October to deal with this matter, and that it would be well for him to be present .at the meeting.

The synod was held in Toronto, and, a number of students having sent in their names, Knox College was founded.

John Black waited over for the opening of the college, which took place on November 5th, 1844, and he may be said to have been its first student. The establishment of this college was a great and notable event, for here many well-known ministers of the Presbyterian Church have been trained for their work. There were two professors to begin with : the polished Henry Esson, who taught arts, and a gentleman from Scotland, Rev. Andrew King, acting professor of theology. Mr. King afterward became professor of theology in Halifax. The beginning of the college was almost as simple as that of the well-known " Log College " which gave instruction in early days to Presbyterian students in the United States. It began in a single room in Professor Esson's house in Toronto. Shelves around the room contained the professor's library and a number of books for the use of the students, lent by other ministers. In the middle of the room was a long pine table, surrounded by benches and a few chairs. Fourteen students received the attention of the two professors. This first session was a busy one, and at its close the enthusiastic young men were sent as home missionaries to different places.

The session was one of great interest to John Black. Well prepared as he had been, a good Greek scholar, well instructed in English literature, and well read in philosophy, he took a foremost place among his fellow-students. Bursaries and prizes were won by him, and the session was thoroughly profitable. Now fairly committed to the Christian ministry, he thought often of the motives which were leading him. His letters of this time show a growing love for spiritual things, and, while there is always in them a spice of humor or of fancy, yet there runs through them a deep and earnest vein.

Among the greatest influences brought to bear upon him were those of the company of good friends, for he was a man of most sociable disposition. In after days he often spoke of the influence of that devoted man of God, William C. Burns, who went as a missionary to China. This remarkable man was a nephew of Dr. Robert Burns, of whom we shall speak more fully, and a friend of Robert Murray McCheyne, one of the most spiritual of the young preachers of his time. Many a story is yet told of the remarkable sayings and doings of William C. Burns during his memorable visit in Canada. His influence, though that of a passing visitor, was very great over the students of Knox College, and over young Black in particular.

At the end of his second year in Knox College the young student was sent as a missionary to preach the Gospel in a number of new settlements. The townships of Brock, Reach, Uxbridge, and Scott were then filling up with immigrants from Great Britain and Ireland. John Black thus writes to his brother :

" Brock, May 27th, 1846.

" I came here about five weeks ago, and have been very busy ever since. I have four preaching stations, two here and two in the next township south. I preach in three schoolhouses and a large barn. The people are mostly Scotch, Irish, and English. The four would make a decent congregation. I take them two each Sabbath, and have prayer-meetings, when I can manage it, as well as week-day 'preachings.' To-morrow night I must ride six miles northwest to hold a meeting among some English people (whom I like best of all my people), and next day, Friday, come back ten miles to a prayer-meeting in another place,

Saturday ten miles again to another, and Sabbath two meetings."

This shows the spirit of the man whose faithful and unremitting services in after years told so powerfully on the banks of the Red River.

A MISSIONARY.

As John Black drew to the end of his college course the work of the ministry became very real to him. His sympathies became more intense in his desire to reach and rescue perishing men. The little band of students in 1846 were all aglow with missionary zeal. The Knox College Missionary Society, which has ever since been so good a training school for young missionaries, was formed in that early time. The society at that date not only did city mission work in Toronto and cultivated the missionary spirit, but helped the Missionary Society of the Free Church of Scotland to support a missionary in a foreign land. During the session of 1846-7 the Rev. Mr. Doudiet, a Swiss Protestant missionary, in the service of the French-Canadian Missionary Society, visited Knox College and addressed the students. The students decided to assist this movement. John Black had, as we have seen, some knowledge of French, and was therefore urged by his fellow-students to enter upon this work. He would have preferred preaching in English, for he had enjoyed his summer in the mission field very greatly, but it was agreed that he should spend the following summer at Pointe aux Trembles, a French school near Montreal, ever since well known. This he did, and returned in the autumn to take his last year in college.

At the opening of this session he was made glad by his brother James joining him from Bovina, to study for the

ministry in Knox College. Not only had he intimate com-
panionship with his brother, but there were three other
students with whom he associated much and of whom he
spoke with the highest regard to the day of his death ; these
were afterward well known as Dr. Robert Ure, of Goderich;
Dr. John Scott, of London ; and the Rev. John Ross, of
Brucefield—all of whom exercised a great influence on the
western peninsula of Upper Canada. He was strongly
attached to his professors. Dr. Burns he regarded as a
fearless champion of the truth ; Professor Esson he admired
for his refined taste and wide scholarship; and Professor
Kintoul, he tells us, he loved as he did his own
father.

FRENCH MISSIONS.

On the close of the college session of 1848 John Black
was ready to enter on the work of the Christian ministry, a
work lying very near to his heart. It seemed, however, as
if it were not to be. The Students' Missionary Society
insisted on his taking a part in the movement among the
French Roman Catholics. He proceeded to Montreal, and
was soon busy studying French. He was not, however, allowed to continue at his work, for there were so
many English-speaking congregations in and about Montreal that he was compelled to take service in these week
after week. This interfered with his plans, and we find him
writing, in 1849, from Pointe aux Trembles : " I left
Montreal and came here about five weeks ago. I have
been making some progress in French, especially in conver-
sation, for it is now the vacation and there are no lessons.
It is a dour (difficult) job. I fear I shall never be able to
use the French effectively."

The estimate in which Mr. Black was held as a preacher

and pastor may be seen from the fact that Côte Street Church, Montreal, the leading Free Church in Canada, having failed to receive continuous help from Scotland, was supplied for months together by the young missionary. He was in request by congregations in different parts of Lower Canada, but he still remained working for the French-Canadians. At length, in May, 1851, he resigned the secretaryship of the French-Canadian Missionary Society. His letters at this time breathe a spirit of earnestness and devotion. He had paid a visit to his former home in New York State, and had seen his old father and mother, and always spoke with the most tender regard of their claims upon him. He was always anxious about the welfare of his brother, to whom he writes. He had then a habit which clung to him to the last, of enquiring minutely into his friends' affairs. His letters abound with direct questions to his brother, such as : "How do you do your work ? Do you sermonize, or expound, or what ? Do you write out your sermons ? Are the professors harmonious in the college? Have you prayer-meetings in college and city ? Do you go out on Sabbaths ? How are you situated for money ?" This habit arose from his warm interest in his friends. His questions at times may have seemed abrupt and forward, but the warmth of his nature showed that it was only " his way."

Three years had now passed in visiting congregations in Canada and the United States, and in preparing himself more fully for his life work, although seriously interrupted by the pressing demands from new congregations. It was a time of great spiritual hope, and the minds of the students of that day had a strong evangelistic bent, which they retained throughout life.

CHAPTER III

Montreal to Fort Garry.

While John Black was wondering what special duty the
Lord would lay upon him he was startled by a cry for help
from the wilds of Rupert's Land.   Forty years before this an
enterprising Scottish nobleman, Lord Selkirk, became a
leading partner in the Hudson's Bay Company, and shortly
after undertook to settle a colony of Highlanders on the
banks of Red River.   The colonists had come in three
separate companies, by way of Hudson Bay, and by a difficult route ascended the water courses to the very heart of
North America, and settled on the banks of Red River.
With true Highland fervor they longed for a minister and a
place of worship.   A Highland elder, James Sutherland,
had accompanied one of the parties, and he had been given
power to marry and baptize.   He had gone east to Canada,
and no minister of their own land had ever come to these
Highland exiles.   As we shall see, a Church of England
minister had been sent to them, and yet they remained
Presbyterian.   After many disappointments their cry had
reached Scotland, and had been referred to Canada to Dr.

Robert Burns, minister of Knox Church, Toronto. We shall enter more fully into the steps they had taken to secure a minister, but at last the Hudson's Bay Company Governor at Fort Garry, Mr. Ballenden, as he was passing through Toronto, had urged the matter upon Dr. Burns. The heart of the good man was touched, and he fixed upon John Black as the missionary. The following extract of a letter to Mr. James Court, the secretary of the French Canadian Missionary Society, speaks for itself :

Toronto, 27th June, 1851.

My Dear Sir,—"In the name of our Synod's Home Mission, and for behoof of our poor brethren at Red River in the Hudson's Bay Territory, I have to solicit your aid in obtaining for a time the services of Mr. John Black, whom we have fixed on as a fit person to make an exploratory visit to the settlement. We would not have asked this could we have avoided it, but our fixed pastors and professors are difficult to move ; and we know Mr. Black's peculiar qualifications. The truth is I was so impressed with the importance of such a visit, both for our people and the red men, and the French speaking settlers in that region, that I gave the pledge as chairman of the committee, and Mr. Ballenden will be entitled to hold me good for it personally, if I cannot get a substitute. If necessary I am ready to resign my charge here and throw myself on the far west, for I am clear that our Church is called to do some good work in those regions ; and if we lose the present opportunity, when may we have another ?

"If you agree, as I trust you will, Mr. Black should come direct to us.

"Most truly yours,
"Robt. Burns.

"Mr. Court, Montreal."

On the following day Dr. Burns wrote a letter to Mr. Black himself. Of this we give a portion :

"Toronto, 28th June, 1851.

"My Dear Sir,—I send you a scroll sketch of instructions, or hints rather, for your guidance in your important mission, *but your own judgment* and good sense will be the best guides.

"You are called at an early period of life to a most important duty, and on the manner in which you shall discharge it will depend, under God, the position which we as a Church may be called upon to occupy in regard to the progress of Christ's kingdom in these western regions. You will find in Bishop Anderson a pious and liberal Episcopalian and a Bishop—yea, *The Bishop!* You know what I mean. Already you know something of Popery and its steps, open or close. The Sabbath observance subject I commend to your serious notice. The company like hunting on the Lord's day! The range is wide and long ; but if you can get from the United States boundary to York Fort, it will be desirable. Your object being exploratory keep note of all. Preach and exhort and expound, and conduct devotional exercises wherever you have an opportunity—Sabbath days especially.

.   .   .   .

"Our prayers will accompany you, and our most fervent desires that your way may be prospered before you, and that you may be hailed by the settlers as a messenger of good tidings and a pioneer of salvation.

"Come up as soon as you can.

"Yours, etc.,

"Robt. Burns."

The young missionary engrossed in his French Canadian work received this communication. He was at the same time earnestly sought for by the congregation of North Georgetown in Lower Canada. After due consideration, he refused Dr. Burns' offer to go to Red River. He did this not because he was lacking in the true spirit of the missionary, but because he felt anxious about his old father and mother still alive in New York State. They were now left without any of their children beside them, and John Black, as their eldest son, felt it to be his duty to be within reach of them. He therefore felt justified in declining the earnest call to visit the Northwest. It is stated that on his refusal application was made to one who has since become known as one of the staunchest theologians and best preachers of the Church, the Rev. Professor MacLaren, D.D., of Knox College, Toronto. He, however, was not able to accept. Very strong pressure was again brought to bear upon John Black, and as the season was advancing his answer had to be given without delay. The following letter written to his brother explains his action in the matter :

ON TO RED RIVER.

Toronto, July 31st, 1851.

MY DEAR JAMES,—" You will no doubt be surprised to learn that I am so far on my way to Red River. I am to be ordained to-night and go on to-morrow morning at half-past seven o'clock. I have been forced into it against my will. It is a very important mission, but I leave one important also, and what grieves me much is that I go without seeing friends—yourself and family at home. Nobody else would go and so I am called on to do so. I shall not be able to return before next spring—be a good boy till I come back.　Write frequently home and comfort them.　I doubt somewhat if I am in the way of duty in leaving father and mother now in their old age.

.　　　　.　　　　.　　　　.

I have no time to write more.　May God bless you and keep you !　Do not cease to pray for my preservation and success and I shall do the same for you.　God bless you, dear brother."

Yours, etc.,

J. BLACK.

P. S.　Now mind you write often home, or if you could possibly go over I should like it very much.　　　　J. B.

On the following day, August 1st, the young missionary who had been ordained for the work of the ministry on the evening before, in Knox Church, Toronto, started on his long journey to Red River.　Twenty years afterward the writer left Toronto for Red River, and could not find before leaving how he was to accomplish the journey after St. Paul, in Minnesota, had been reached.　How much more difficult when the long journey of eight hundred miles to St. Paul had to be performed over bad roads by stage coach and Mississippi steamboat !　The journey that now takes thirty hours from Toronto, *via* Detroit, Chicago, and St. Paul, then took two full weeks.　The young missionary arrived at where the city of Minneapolis now stands, and wrote the following letter.

Falls of St. Anthony, August 15th, 1851.

DEAR JAMES : " I am so far on my way and hope to begin another stage of my journey on Monday next.　My journey has yet been comparatively pleasant, though diversified with a good deal of the disagreeable, owing chiefly to bad roads and anxiety as to being too late. I am, however, here and well, and hope to get through. Pray for strength and protection and faithfulness and success. There is now to be a regular monthly mail and so I hope you will write regularly. The mail starts from here on the 1st of the month. To be in time you must post in the middle of the month previous. I add no more at present. May God bless and keep you evermore. Do not forget me at a throne of Grace."

Yours, etc.,

JOHN BLACK.

When the traveller reached the capital of Minnesota he was in the greatest perplexity. His coming had been anxiously looked for by a deputation of the Scottish settlers from Red River. But they were nearly five hundred miles from home and a tedious cart journey lay before them, so that the time of the year did not permit their delaying any longer. On the 1st of August, just at the time their long-looked-for missionary was leaving Toronto, the deputation left the Falls of St. Anthony to return to Red River.

A FRIEND IN NEED.

At this most important point a happy deliverance came to the young missionary. He learned that Alexander Ramsey, the Governor of Minnesota, was soon to set out to the north of Minnesota, attended with a mounted escort. Governor Ramsey had organized the territory of Minnesota two years before, and had the year before negotiated a treaty with the Sioux Indians, by which they ceded a large tract of land in southern Minnesota. He was now to proceed

3

northward to Pembina, to make a treaty with the Chip-
pewa Indians.   Mr. Black, though, as he tells us, at a considerable expense to himself, was given the privilege of
going to his northern home along with this party.

We are fortunate in having two camp-fire sketches written
by Mr. J. W. Bond, who was also one of the party.   He
tells us that the party met from several different points
near the Sauk rapids, on the Upper Mississippi.   Besides
the governor and his staff there were Rev. John Black and
Mr. Bond.   The escort consisted of twenty-five dragoons
from Fort Snelling, commanded by an American military
officer, and accompanied by six two-horse baggage wagons.   The baggage of the party and the provisions were
carried in light Red River carts, with eight French-Canadian
and halfbreed drivers.   In number there were comprised
about fifty souls in all.   John Black and Mr. Bond, each
mounted on an Indian pony, became companions during
the journey, and Mr. Black won the regard of all the members of the party.

EN ROUTE.

We may give a few notes of the journey over the prairies :

Sauk Rapids, August 21st, 1851 :   " Fine, clear, cool
day.   We struck tents and went away early.   Passed over
the worst piece of road between the Rapids and Pembina.
The dragoons were busy for several hours in repairing the
'corduroy' for the passage of the teams."

August 23rd :   " We to-day rode over the rolling prairie,
full of strips of marsh, when, after a march of ten miles,
we came to an almost impassable swamp.   We crossed
with some difficulty by pulling the carts and horses across
by ropes, during which Rev. Mr. Black and Mr. Bond completely mired their ponies, and came near going with them

to the bottom, if there was any. After this we took a cup of tea to refresh ourselves."

August 24th (Sunday). "To-day our French-Canadians and halfbreeds, who have charge of the provision and baggage carts, have been shooting pigeons and ducks, and also making new cart axles. The day has not seemed much like Sunday."

August 25th. "Mosquitoes are very bad, although the weather is quite cold and bracing."

August 26th. "We had a very good dinner to day, consisting of bouillon (broth) made of geese, ducks, etc., with ham, pork, coffee, bread and butter, etc."

August 27th. "Cool, cloudy, and quite cold early in the morning; fine weather for travelling; up at daylight, and away upon our march at half-past five. We are to-day passing on the dividing ridge between the head waters of the Red, Minnesota, and Mississippi rivers."

August 30th. "To-day suffered much from mosquitoes. No imagination can do them justice—they must be seen and felt to be appreciated. Mr. Bond rode a cream-colored horse, and declared that he was unable to distinguish the color of the animal, so thickly was he covered with the pests. During supper they swarmed around like bees living, and entered the mouth, nose, eyes, and ears, and had it not been for a cool fresh evening breeze they would have been unbearable."

August 31st. "Our hunters discovered two buffalo bulls about two miles ahead. They immediately equipped and started, and soon surrounded and killed both. We soon joined them and encamped. The buffaloes were skinned, the choice parts cut out, and the liver and kidney fried for dinner. These were our first buffaloes, and there was much excitement over them."

September 1st. "Another buffalo to-day, but a sad accident. During the chase Pierre Bottineau, our best French halfbreed guide, was thrown violently from his horse, which stumbled. Bottineau was picked up insensible, terribly stunned, though not much hurt. He was bled, brought to camp in the carriage and put to bed."

September 4th. "The prairie is so bare that no wood is to be had. Having no wood we were obliged to boil our kettle, and the French boys their pork and buffalo, over a fire made of buffalo chips, *i.e.*, of dried buffalo manure picked up on the prairie. Only a few mosquitoes troubled us, and they were driven to leeward by the strong smoke and smell of the buffalo chips."

September 6th. "To-night there was the finest exhibition of the *aurora borealis* that any of us have ever seen. To attempt a description is the height of vanity. The Rev. Mr. Black and Mr. Bond gazed very long upon it, as a most remarkable manifestation in the heavens, before they could tear themselves away and return to rest. Mr. Black, who had seen the Northern sky in Scotland and Canada, says it was much the finest exhibition he has ever seen. Bottineau declared that he had never seen its equal this side of Hudson Bay."

September 7th. "It is three weeks to-day since we left St. Paul."

September 8th. "A furious thunderstorm overtook us. It came down a deluge, a perfect torrent of falling waters, though the heaviest of the storm had passed around us to the south."

September 11th. "Arrived at Pembina". The houses were full of halfbreeds, who saluted us with the discharge of guns, etc. Two of the staff rode on ahead, and were treated to milk and potatoes—a treat equal to that of the milk and honey received by the Israelites of old. Near the village, on the muddy banks of Red River, stood an admiring group of several hundred whites, halfbreeds, and Indians of all sizes, with any quantity of dogs, very large and wolfish. Amid this babel of cries, yelps, barks, and shouts, from the said big dogs and little papoose Indians, we came to a halt and reconnoitred, standing almost glued fast in the sticky, tenacious mud caused by the rains and overflow of the Red and Pembina Rivers for three years past. The journey to Pembina has been accomplished, including the two rest days, in twenty-five days in all."

September 14th. "Cloudy, cold, raw, and windy, quite unpleasant and unseasonable. An overcoat is necessary out of doors this morning, and fires in the house for comfort. To-day we had preaching by the Rev. John Black, in the dining-room of the Governor's house ; a novelty most certainly in this far distant region. The congregation consisted of about a dozen whites and three halfbreeds. The Rev. Charles Tanner, a halfbreed missionary among the Indians of Red Lake, met us here, and in the afternoon preached to the assembled Chippewas in their own tongue. He moved to this place a week ago, and intends farming, teaching school, etc., for a livelihood after the conclusion of the treaty. His wife is a halfbreed, and they reside at present in a lodge in the yard at this place."

DOWN THE RED RIVER.

After Sunday was past for two days the weather was bad, but on Wednesday, 17th, the day was fine, and the two companions of the voyage, Messrs. Black and Bond, determined to leave the party behind and proceed down the Red River to the Selkirk settlement, a distance by land of sixty miles, but not less than three times as far by the winding river. Astir by daylight, the travellers were soon ready, and in a birch bark canoe, fifteen feet long and three wide, managed by two French halfbreeds or Bois-brulés (burnt sticks, referring to their dusky faces), their bedding, baggage, and provisions, and finally the two passengers were stowed away for the journey. The voyage was a tedious one, but not without interest. The canoe was somewhat leaky, and at times had to be hauled up on the bank, overturned, emptied, and calked with white spruce gum. Large flocks of ducks and geese were swimming almost within paddle length from the canoe. Everywhere were to be seen traces of the high water which had prevailed for several years, and marks upon the trees thirty feet above the water were seen, where in spring the freshets had reached.

A NIGHT SCENE.

The party halted for the night some forty miles below Pembina. The description given by Mr. Black's travelling companion of the camp on the river bank is graphic : " The night is very clear and fine, the face of heaven is smiling amid myriads of twinkling stars ; the northern horizon is lit up with the rays of dancing beams of an aurora, while the woods and silent-flowing river are illuminated by our camp fire ; our voyageurs are fast asleep upon the ground before us, and not a sound is heard save that of the leaping, crackling flames and the low tone of our own voices as we chat merrily. And now, as my companion reads a chapter in his French pocket Bible, and I pencil down these sketches of fact and fancy by the light of the burning fagots—but hark ! we have company, it seems, and are not so lonely as I thought ; that was the hoot-owl's cry, and sounds like the wailing of a fiend in misery ; that was the cry, long drawn out and dismal, of a distant wolf; and near, the pack like hungry curs are heard yelping and barking furiously. In the bushes beside the camp I see two gleaming, fiery eye-balls. "Take that, to light you to better quarters ! " I hurl a blazing firebrand toward the beast, who, with a dismal cry, leaves us to repose and quiet sleep."

Another day and still another night of camping, and next morning the party start on the home stretch. With a head wind the voyageurs toiled on, and both passengers relieved the monotony by landing on the right bank, walking along it, and cutting off the bends kept ahead of the canoe. During the day they found by the appearance of houses along the banks that they were approaching their destination. The vivid description given by Mr. Bond fell, in some way, into the hands of the American poet, Whittier, and he has left us a sweet poem, with which we should be acquainted The scene is that of the voyageurs coming down the stream, and as they approach their destination there is first the sound of bells, and then the sight of the Roman Catholic Cathedral of St. Boniface with the two towers.

A picture much like this was seen as the voyageurs in the old days left Ste. Anne on the Ottawa, not far from Montreal, and took their leave, under the protection of Providence, for their long journey to the interior. Thomas Moore, the Irish poet, was much impressed by the sight, on his visit to Canada, when he wrote the Canadian boat song :

"Faintly as tolls the evening chime,
Our voices keep tune and our oars keep time."

So the weary voyageurs approaching St. Boniface are
filled with expectation and delight at the end of their
journey by the cheery chimes of the Roman Mission.

THE RED RIVER VOYAGEUR

Out and in the river is winding
    The links of its long red chain,
Through belts of dusky pine land
    And gusty leagues of plain.

Only at times a smoke wreath
    With the drifting cloud-rack joins—
The smoke of the hunting lodges
    Of the wild Assiniboins !

Drearily blows the north-wind
    From the land of ice and snow ;
The eyes that look are weary,
    And heavy the hands that row.

And with one foot on the water,
    And one upon the shore,
The Angel of Shadow gives warning,
    That day shall be no more.

Is it the clang of wild geese ?
    Is it the Indians' yell,
That lends to the voice of the north-wind
    The tones of a far-off bell ?

The voyageur smiles as he listens
    To the sound that grows apace ;
Well he knows the vesper ringing
    Of the bells of St. Boniface.

The bells of the Roman Mission
    That call from their turrets twain ;
To the boatman on the river,
    To the hunter on the plain !

The bells of the Roman Mission,
That call from their turrets twain;
To the boatman on the river,
To the hunter on the plain:

Even so in our mortal journey
  The bitter north-winds blow,
And thus upon life's Red River
  Our hearts, as oarsmen, row.

And when the Angel of Shadow
  Rests his feet on wave and shore,
And our eyes grow dim with watching,
  And our hearts faint at the oar,

Happy is he who heareth
  The signal of his release
In the bells of the Holy City,
  The chimes of eternal peace !

In the afternoon the party disembarked and found a
kindly shelter in the hospitable home of an old French
family, the Marions, not far from the cathedral, opposite
the point where the Assiniboine falls into the Red River,
and the stone walls of Fort Garry in view in the distance.

CHAPTER IV

A Highland Welcome.

A short rest having been made in the hospitable home of the Marions, the young missionary, anxious to meet his future flock, crossed the Red River by canoe and disembarked about a mile below, at "Colony Gardens." This was the house of Alexander Ross, sheriff of Assiniboia, who had been a leader in all the efforts to obtain a minister. Here the expected minister received a Highland welcome, and the Ross mansion became his home.

A short sketch of Sheriff Ross and his wife is an absolute necessity to our understanding of the Red River community to which John Black came. Alexander Ross was a Highlander who, about 1803, at the age of twenty-one, came with the disbanded soldiers of the Highland regiment of Glengarry Fencibles to Upper Canada. He went with them to Glengarry District on the St. Lawrence, and, being a fair scholar, taught school there for some time.

In 1810 he entered the Astor Fur Company, which had its headquarters in New York. Sailing from that city, he rounded Cape Horn, went up the Pacific coast, and helped to build Astoria, a fort at the mouth of the Columbia river, on the Pacific. He led a rough and dangerous life for a number of years, and found his way in the service of the Northwest Fur Company of Montreal, to the mountains of British Columbia. Here he married an Indian maiden, the daughter of the chief of the Okanagan Indians. The writer was well acquainted, many years after, with " Granny " Ross, as she was called, and can speak of her kindness and Christian character.

At the end of the first quarter of the century Alexander Ross was brought across the mountains and prairies by Governor George Simpson, and took up his abode on the banks of Red River, on what is now the site of the city of Winnipeg. Here he reared a large family, and took a lead-ing part in all tne affairs of the Red River settlement. Mr. Black's companion writes : "The old gentleman met us on the bank, welcomed us to the Selkirk settlement, and escorted us up to his house—a white, rough-cast, two-storey stone, which stands upon a large bend of the river and commands a view both ways ; and that view is cer-tainly the finest I have seen for a long time."

The scene about Colony Gardens on that September afternoon was a very striking one. " A village of farm-houses with barns, stables, hay, wheat, and barley stooks, with small cultivated fields or lots, well fenced, are stretch-ing along the meandering river, while the prairies, far off to the horizon, are covered over with herds of cattle, horses, etc., the fields filled with a busy throng of whites, half-breeds, and Indians—men, squaws, and children—all reap-ing, binding, and stacking the golden grain, while hundreds of carts, with a single horse or ox harnessed in their shafts, are brought in requisition to carry it to the well-stored barn, and are seen moving, with their immense loads rolling

along like huge stacks in all directions. Add to this the
numerous wind-mills, some in motion, whirling around
their giant arms, while others, motionless, are waiting for a
grist. Just above, Fort Garry sits in the angle at the junction of the Assiniboine and Red rivers, with a blood-red
flag inscribed with the letters ' H. B. Co.' floating gaily in
the breeze."

Of the house of Sheriff Ross the writer says : " We spent
the night with Mr. Ross and family, and found him to be a
very intelligent and interesting old gentleman, full of information as regards the Northwest region, and of Selkirk
colony in particular. He published a book descriptive of
the country and of the Rocky Mountains, Vancouver and
the Pacific Coast, where he spent some fifteen years
of his life, since which he has been residing in this
colony, and has been for a long time one of its leading
citizens."

A book entitled " Red River Settlement," published by
Sheriff Ross, some years after this time, is really a lively
and correct account in most respects of the Selkirk colony.
We have gleaned from his writings, and from the information communicated to Dr. Burns by him, the main facts
leading up to the coming of John Black to the Highland
colony. No doubt, late into that first night, the religious
story of the forty years preceding, was told by the old fur
trader to the youthful missionary. We may well rehearse
the tale of disappointment now to be turned to joy.

The Scottish settlers of Red River were chiefly emigrants from the north of Scotland, brought to the country
during and before the year 1815, by the Earl of Selkirk.
They had a clergyman of their own persuasion promised by
his lordship at the time of leaving their native country, the

Rev. Mr. Sage, but he remained behind them for a year in order to perfect himself in the Gaelic language. He was expected to follow them. Next year, however, came and passed away and with it no clergyman ; and up to the time of Mr. Black's coming no Presbyterian minister had ever visited Rupert's Land. In the winter of 1815-16 the settlers had to abandon the colony for want of food, and they betook themselves to the plains for buffalo, and to the lakes for fish, and wintered among the natives in all directions. In 1816, after their return to the settlement, they were driven from the colony at the muzzle of the gun by the Northwest fur traders, who did not want a farming settlement in Rupert's Land, and they spent the following winter three hundred miles to the north of the colony, at the foot of Lake Winnipeg.

Led by the vicissitudes of his settlers, Lord Selkirk visited his colony in 1817, made a treaty with the Indians, and made promises to his settlers, among other things, to send them a minister of their own faith. Much encouraged by his lordship's visit, the people settled down to work, when they were invaded by a grasshopper scourge, and had been compelled again to leave their farms and seek subsistence by the chase of the buffalo on the plains.

At this juncture (1818) they were surprised at the arrival of two Roman Catholic priests sent from Montreal, on the request of Lord Selkirk, for the Roman Catholic colonists taken out by him, and the French halfbreeds of Red River. But no Presbyterian minister was sent. It is to be said for Lord Selkirk that the financial difficulties of his colony and the strife and opposition which had arisen preyed on his mind to such an extent that he died in the south of France in 1820. He had, however, given strict charges to his agent, then in London, to send out a minister as promised. The agent was an Englishman and seemed to have used his position with the directors of the Hudson Bay Company very unfairly. In 1820 there arrived in Red River Rev. John West, a good and suitable man, but the settlers complained that he was of the Church of England, and that there were not "twenty individuals in the whole colony belonging to the Church of England."

Much dissatisfied, the colonists, in 1822, applied to Lord Selkirk's executors for redress, but no answer was made to them. Governor Donald Mackenzie, who was in charge at Fort Garry, made them, in the year following, a promise that a minister of their own persuasion would be sent them. A petition sent to Scotland for assistance received no reply. Years rolled on, the people still adhering in their homes to the customs of their fathers, holding prayer meetings from house to house and teaching the Shorter Catechism in their families. In 1843 they saw six Roman Catholic priests in the settlement, and four Church of England ministers, but none of their own faith.

The state of depression produced by these unavailing efforts may be seen in the fact that in 1835 a party of one hundred and ten persons, all Scotch settlers, left the colony for the United States, "solely because at the Selkirk settlement they had neither minister nor church of their own." Two years after a number of additional families left the country for the same reason. The indiscreet and uncalled for public address of one of their ministers, who had been once a Presbyterian but was so no longer, did much to influence their feeling and stir up resentment.

In the year 1844, Duncan Finlayson, a Scotchman, who was Governor at Fort Garry, advised another application to be made to the company in London. The petition of the people is really a most pathetic one. In it they say that " they are in danger of forgetting that they have brought with them into this land, where they have sought a home, nothing so valuable as the faith of Christ, or the primitive simplicity of their form of worship; and that their children are in danger of losing sight of those Christian bonds of union and of worship, which everywhere characterize the sincere follower of Christ."

In reply to this petition, the company denied any promise of Lord Selkirk to the settlers in the matter, but agreed to pay the expenses of a minister of their own faith to the country, provided they were willing to undertake his support. Again stirred up to vindicate their position, the leaders made affidavits as to Lord Selkirk's promise in their old Highland home of Helmsdale, in Sutherlandshire, before the Colonists emigrated, as well as at the time in 1817 when His Lordship gave the grant of land for church and school. The response to these declarations from the Hudson's Bay Company was no more satisfactory than the former had been, and thus ended the expectation which the Kildonan people had fondly cherished for more than thirty years of having a minister sent them by the company.

Now that they had learned the wisdom of the admonition —" Put not your trust in princes," the disappointed colonists began to turn their thoughts to the sympathy of the Scottish people. In 1846 they addressed a letter to the Free Church of Scotland, which in the following year reached the Colonial Committee of that Church. This committee sought in vain to obtain a minister for Red River, in Scotland, and in turn, through Dr. Bonar, the convener of the committee, handed the matter over to the Free Church in Canada.

Then the persistent settlers of Red River transferred their case to Montreal, and wrote to Sir George Simpson, who has been called the " Emperor of Rupert's Land," and asked for his countenance and support. Though very diplomatic, Sir George seems to have favored them. An interesting correspondence between Rev. Mr. Rintoul, of Montreal, and Sir George, now took place. The work of obtaining a suitable missionary was, as we have seen, in the hands of Rev. Dr. Robert Burns, of Knox Church, Toronto, a relative of Dr. Bonar. Chief Factor Ballenden, resident governor at Fort Garry, took much interest in the matter, and pressed the case of the Red River settlers on Dr. Burns and his committee. We have already seen the steps by which the apostle of Red River was sent upon his way.

Mr. Black had faced the journey, and now on the scene of his future labors heard the details of the well-nigh forty years of disappointment, as well as of the Highland wel. come awaiting him. The joy that took possession of the Highland hearts of the people of Red River was almost beyond measure. They had unremittingly striven in the face of many rebuffs for a pure Gospel and for the coming of the house of the Lord. And now in many of the homes of Red River at their family worship they sang :

When Sion's bondage God turned back
As men that dreamed were we,
Then filled with laughter was our mouth,
Our tongue with melody.

As streams of water in the south,
Our bondage, Lord, recall.
Who sow in tears a reaping time
Of joy enjoy they shall.

That man who, bearing precious seed,
  In going forth doth mourn,
He doubtless bringing back his sheaves,
  Rejoicing shall return.

It was Friday afternoon when John Black arrived at his
destination on Red River.   On Sabbath following he went
with the people to the Episcopal Church of St. John's, now
on the north side of the city of Winnipeg, in which the
Kildonan people always claimed a share.   Expecting their
minister, the people had made a compromise with the Hudson's Bay Company as to property, and had been given a
glebe lot called "La Grenouilliere," Frog Plain, two or three
miles down the river, as a site for church and manse.
Here they had already erected a manse for their new minister, and though not quite finished, it served as a meeting-
place for the people in their worship for the first year or
two of the mission.

During the week after Mr. Black's arrival, the news
went quickly about the settlement, so that on Sabbath,
September 28th, 1851, three hundred of the Selkirk settlers,
who had a week before met in St. John's, assembled for
service in the manse at Kildonan.   Here the first sermon
was preached by a Presbyterian minister in the wide region
west of Lake Superior, where now the Presbyterian Church
is much the largest body engaged in spreading the Gospel.

CHAPTER V

The Early Settlers on Red River.

On the banks of the Red River of the North for well nigh forty years before the coming of John Black, there had existed the Red River Settlement. Fort Garry was its centre for upwards of thirty years of that period. The fur trader on the Mackenzie River looked to the settlement as his probable haven of rest when he should have finished his days of active service and retired; the half-breed hunter of the plains thought of it as the paradise to which he might make his annual visit, or the place where he might at last settle, while the Kildonan settler boasted that there was no place like his "oasis" in the Northwest wilderness, and that the traveller who had tasted the magical waters of Red River would always return to them again. The Canadian youth read in his school-book of a far distant outpost, Fort Garry, and chilled by the very sound of the name, whispering "cold as Siberia," passed on to the next subject. The Canadian statesman dreamed of a Canada from ocean to ocean, but as he thought of the thousand miles of impass-able rocks and morasses between him and the fur-traders, he could only shudder and say, "perhaps sometime," while the secretary of the Hudson's Bay Company House in London with darkest secrecy folded together his epistles, addressed them "*via* Pembina," and then slipped quietly away to his suburban residence, knowing that he had the key in his pocket to unlock the door to half a continent, around which was built an impenetrable Chinese wall.

As early as 1802 the Earl of Selkirk, a man of philanthropic and liberal views, stirred by the accounts given by Sir Alexander Mackenzie (1801) and other traders to the Indian country, wrote to the British Government of the day a letter now in the British archives, proposing the establishment in Red River of a colony for the purpose of relieving Irish disaster and Highland misery. It was not until 1811 that Lord Selkirk succeeded in obtaining, by purchase from the Hudson's Bay Company, of which in the meantime he had become a member, the district of Assiniboia on Red River, comprising 116,000 square miles. By way of Hudson Bay was the route chosen, and in the letters of the founder occur the words—words of still unfulfilled, but no doubt true prophecy : "To a colony in these territories the channel of trade must be the river of Port Nelson."

THE HIGHLANDERS.

At this time (1811) there were sad times in the Highlands of Scotland. Cottars and crofters were being driven from their small holdings by the Duchess of Sutherland and others, to make way for large sheep farms. Strong men stood sullenly by, women wept, and wrung their hands, and children clung to their distressed parents as they saw their steadings burnt before their eyes. The " Highland clearances " have left a stain on the escutcheons of more than one nobleman. Lord Selkirk, whose estates were in the south of Scotland, and who had no special connection with the Celts, nevertheless took pity on the helpless Highland exiles. Ships were prepared, and the following are the numbers of Highland colonists sent out in the respective years :

In 1811, reaching Red River in 1812, there were....... 70
In 1812, reaching Red River in 1813, there were (a part Highland)............... .... 15 or 20
In 1813, reaching Red River in 1814, there were....... 93
In 1815, reaching Red River in the same year, there were 100
———
Total Selkirk Highland colonists, about 270

The names of these settlers were those still well known in Manitoba, as Sutherland, McKay, McLeod, McPherson, Matheson, Macdonald, Livingstone, Polson, McBeth, Bannerman, and Gunn.

From the above list it will be seen that at the end of 1814 the colony had reached the number of one hundred and eighty or two hundred. Over these ruled the Hudson's Bay Company governor, Capt. Miles Macdonell, a U. E. Loyalist from Glengarry, in Canada. The fact that the Highland settlers were under the protection of the Hudson's Bay Company roused against them the opposition of the Northwest Fur Company, of Montreal, which had for thirty or forty years before their coming carried on trade in the country.

The two companies had their rival posts side by side at many points throughout the Territories. The Nor'wester fort standing immediately at the junction of the Red and Assiniboine rivers was called Fort Gibraltar. The fort occupied by the colony was less than a mile down the bank of the Red River, and was known as Fort Douglas from Lord Selkirk's family name. It is of no consequence to our present object to determine who opened hostilities or who was to blame in the contest of the companies. Strife prevailed, and through this the colonists suffered. In 1814 arrived on the scene a jauntily-dressed officer of the Nor'-west Company, brandishing a sword and signing himself captain—one Duncan Cameron. This man was a clever, diplomatic, and rather unscrupulous instrument of his company, and coming to command Fort Gibraltar, cultivated the colonists, spoke Gaelic to and entertained them with much hospitality, and ended by inducing about one hundred and fifty of the two hundred of them to desert Red River and go with him to Upper Canada. By a long and wearisome journey to Fort William, and then in small boats along Lakes Superior and Huron, they reached Penetanguishene, and found new homes near Toronto, London, and elsewhere. To the faithful half hundred who remained true to their pledges all honor is due.

The arrival of the third party of Highlanders in 1815 reinforced the remnant who had resisted Cameron's seductive proposals. The Colony again rose to three-fourths its original strength. In 1816 the Nor'westers adopted still more extreme measures to destroy the colony. An attack was made on the settlers on the 19th of June, and the new Governor, Robert Semple, was killed, with a number of his attendants, at a spot a short distance north of the present city of Winnipeg. Lord Selkirk on the receipt of the news of the colony in 1815 had come to Montreal, and was proceeding up the lakes to assist his people in 1816, when the news reached him, on the way, of the skirmish of " Seven Oaks " and the death of the governor. He was at the very time bringing with him as settlers, a number of disbanded soldiers, who have usually been known as the " De Meurons."

The regiments to which these men belonged were part of the body of German mercenaries which had been raised during the Napoleonic wars. The name of Col. De Meuron, one of the principal officers, was given to the whole.

These new settlers were not all Germans, but had among them a number of Swiss and Piedmontese. The regiments had been employed by Britain in the war of 1812-15, and were disbanded in Montreal at its close. Lord Selkirk engaged four officers and one hundred men to go to Red River. The men were promised certain wages, as well as land grants at Red River. In the autumn of 1816 the party arrived at Fort William, which they seized and the camping place on the Kaministiquia River is still called Point De Meuron. Employed during the winter in opening out for a distance a military road, the party under command of Capt. D'Orsonnens in early spring pushed on by the way of the western shore of the Lake of the Woods, surprised the Northwesters, and retook Fort Douglas from them. Lord Selkirk arrived at the Red River in the last week of June, 1817. In accordance with his agreement he settled all the De Meurons who wished to remain, along the banks of the little river, the Seine, which empties into the Red River opposite Point Douglas. This stream has among the old settlers always been known as German Creek in consequence. Being mostly Roman Catholics they were the first settlers among whom the priests Provencher and Dumoulin took up their abode on their arrival in 1818. From the nationality of the De Meurons the first Roman Catholic parish formed in the country was called St. Boniface, from Winifred, or Boniface, the German apostle and patron saint. The first Roman Catholic parish is now the town of St. Boniface, and is the residence of the Roman Catholic Archbishop of the country.

Some severe things have been said of the character of
the De Meuron settlers. They have been charged with
turbulence, insobriety, and with having had predatory in-
clinations towards their neighbours' cattle. They almost
all left the country after the disastrous year of 1826, for the
United States. No doubt like all bodies of men they had
good and bad among them, but the fact of their having
been disbanded mercenaries would not incline us to expect
a very high morality of them.

THE SWISS.

In the same year (1820) in which Lord Selkirk went to
France, to find, in the little town of Pau, his death and
burial place, a former officer of a disbanded regiment—Col.
May—a native of the Swiss capital of Berne, went as an
agent of Lord Selkirk to Switzerland. He had been in
Canada, but not at Red River, and accordingly his repre-
sentations among the Swiss Cantons were too much of the
kind circulated by Government emigration agents still. He
succeeded in inducing a considerable number of Swiss
families to seek the Red River settlement. Crossing the
ocean by Hudson's Bay Company ships, they arrived at
York Factory in August, 1821, and were borne in York
boats to their destination.

Gathered, as they had been, from the towns and villages
of Switzerland, and being chiefly " watch and clock makers,
pastry cooks, and musicians," they were ill-suited for such a
new settlement as that of Red River, where they must become agriculturists. They seem to have been honest and
orderly people, though very poor. It will be remembered
that the De Meurons had come as soldiers; they were
chiefly, therefore, unmarried men. The arrival of the
Swiss, with their handsome daughters, produced a flutter

of excitement in the wifeless DeMeuron cabins along German creek. The results may be described in the words of a most trustworthy eye-witness of what took place : " No sooner had the Swiss emigrants arrived than many of the Germans, who had come to the settlement a few years ago from Canada, and had houses, presented themselves in search of a wife, and, having fixed their attachment with acceptance, they received those families in which was their choice into their habitations. Those who had no daughters to afford this introduction were obliged to pitch their tents along the banks of the river and outside the stockades of the fort, till they removed to Pembina in better prospects of provisions for the winter."

THE METIS.

Alongside the Selkirk settlers others began to settle on the vacant banks of Red River. Most worthy of notice among them were the half-breeds of French or English descent, whose mothers were Indian women.

Parkman, in his account of Pontiac's conspiracy, has well shown the facility with which the French voyageurs and Indian people coalesced. Though a poor colonist, the French-Canadian is unequalled as a voyageur and pioneer runner. When he settles on a remote lake or untenanted river, he is at home. Here he rears in contentment his " dusky race." The French half-breed, called also Metis, and formerly Bois-brulé, is an athletic, rather good-looking, lively, excitable, easy going being. Fond of a fast pony, fond of merry-making, free-hearted, open-handed, yet indolent and improvident, he is a marked feature of border life. Being excitable, he can be aroused to acts of revenge, of bravery, and daring. The McGillivrays, Grants, McLeods, and Mackays, who had French, Scotch, and Indian blood, were especially determined.

The Metis, if a friend, is true, and cannot in too many ways oblige you.

The offspring of the Montreal traders with their Indian spouses, so early as 1816, numbered several hundreds, and they possessed a considerable esprit-de-corps. They looked upon themselves as a separate people, and, headed by their Scoto-French half-breed leader, Cuthbert Grant, called themselves the New Nation. Having tasted blood in the death of Governor Semple, they were turbulent ever after. Living the life of buffalo hunters, they preserved their war-like tastes. Largely increased in numbers in 1849, they committed the grave offence of rising, taking the law into their own hands, defying all authority, and rescuing a French half-breed prisoner named Sayer.

This was in the time of Recorder Thom. Adam Thom, the judge, deserves a word of notice. A native of Scotland, of large frame, great intelligence, and strong will, he had had experience as a journalist in Montreal. Sent up to establish law and order, he certainly did his best, and should have had a proper force to support him. True, exception has been taken to his decisions, but where is the judge that escapes that?

Among the leaders in this affair was one with the ominous name of Riel, a Scoto-French half-breed, who owned a mill on the Seine River. He was the father of Louis Riel who afterwards led the French half-breeds in their two rebellions. Louis Riel, the younger, was the embodiment of the restless spirit of his race. Ambitious, vain, capable of inspiring confidence in the breasts of the ignorant, yet violent, vacillating and vindictive, the rebel chieftain died to atone for the turbulence of his people.

ENGLISH HALF BREEDS.

As different as is the patient roadster from the wild mus-
tang, is the English-speaking half-breed from the Metis.
So early as 1775 the traveller, Alexander Henry, found
Orkney employees in the service of the Hudson's Bay
Company at Cumberland House. The Orkney Islands
furnished so many useful men to the company that in 1816,
when the Bois-brulés came to attack the colony, though the
colonists were mostly Highlanders, they were called "Les
Orcanais." Since 1821 the same supply of employees to
the company has continued and increased with occasionally
an admixture of Caithness-shire and other Highlanders.

Accordingly the English-speaking half-breeds are almost
entirely of Scotch descent. From Hudson's Bay to distant
Yukon the steady-going Orkney men have come with their
Indian wives and half-breed children and made the Red
River their home. We have but to mention such well-
known respectable names as Inkster, Fobister, Setter,
Harper, Mowat, Omand, Flett, Linklater, Tait, Spence,
Monkman, and others, to show how valuable an element of
population the English half-breeds have been, though, of
course, there are those bearing these names as well who are
of pure Orkney blood.

HUDSON'S BAY COMPANY OFFICERS.

No element, however, did so much for Red River of old
as the intelligent and high-spirited officers of the Hudson's
Bay Company, of whom many settled in the country
There was among them also a strong Highland and Orkney strain. In few countries is the speech of the people
generally so correct as it was in the Red River settlement. This undoubtedly arose from the influence of the
educated Hudson's Bay Company officers. At their distant

posts on the long nights they read useful books and kept their journals. Numbers of them collected specimens of natural history, Indian curiosities, took meteorological observations, and the like. Though all may not have been the pink of perfection, yet very few bodies of men retained, as a whole, so upright a character as they. We have but to mention such names as that of the notable governor, Sir George Simpson, of Pruden, Bird, Bunn, Stewart, Lillie, Campbell, Christie, Kennedy, Heron, Ross, Murray, MacKenzie, Hardisty, Graham, McTavish, Bannatyne, Cowan, Rowand, Sinclair, Sutherland, Finlayson, Smith, Balsillie, McLean, McFarlane, and Hargrave, and others who have settled on the Red River, to establish this.

THE PENSIONERS.

Most portions of the new world have grown from additions from the military, who have for some reason or other come to them. So it was in Red River settlement. In 1846 the 6th Regiment of foot, some three hundred and fifty strong, was sent out by way of Hudson's Bay under Col. Crofton, in connection with the Oregon question, then disturbing the relations of Great Britain and the United States. Few of the regiment remained in the country. The troublous state of affairs in Recorder Thom's time induced the company to send out a number of pensioners and settlers who should be settled near the fort, and be useful in time of emergency as police. It was in 1848 that Col. Caldwell, with fifty-six non-commissioned officers and men, of whom forty-two were married and had families, came out by way of Hudson's Bay, each man being promised twenty acres of land and each sergeant forty. It was after their arrival that the Sayer emeute took place.

THE CENSUS.

The nucleus of 150 Kildonan settlers in 1816 had with it a few Metis, already settled down, but there was a need for a settlement for the heart of the vast fur territories. The North-west Company, ever opposed to settlement, we learn from Harmon's book, had a scheme on foot at this time to establish a native settlement on Rainy River, and had the money subscribed for an educational institution there. A settlement having been once established on Red River, many flocked to it. Thus it was that in ten years after the death of Governor Semple there were of Highlanders, De Meurons, Swiss, French voyageurs, Metis, and Orkney half-breeds, not less than fifteen hundred settlers. It was certainly a motley throng. The Rev. Mr. West the first missionary, tells us that he distributed copies of the Bible in English, Gaelic, German, Danish, Italian, and French, and they were all gratefully received in this polygot community. Though the colony lost by desertion, as we have seen, yet it continued to gain by the addition of retiring Hudson's Bay Company officers and servants, who took up land, as allowed by the company, in strips along the river, after the Lower Canadian fashion, for which they paid small sums. There were in many cases no deeds, simply the registration of the name in the company's register. A man sold his lot for a horse, and it was a matter of chance whether the registration of the change in the lot took place or not. This was certainly a mode of transferring land free enough to suit the greatest radical. The land reached as far out from the river as could be seen by looking under a horse, say two miles, and back of this was the limitless prairie, which became a species of common where all could cut hay, and where herds could run unconfined.

Wood, water and hay, were the three r's of a Red River settler's life ; to cut poplar rails for his fences in spring and burn the dried rails in the following winter was quite the proper thing. There was no inducement to grow surplus grain, as each settler could only get a market for eight bushels of wheat from the Hudson's Bay Company. It could not be exported. Pemican from the plains was easy to get ; the habits of the people were simple, their wants were few, and while the picture was hardly Arcadian, yet the new order of things since that time has borne pretty severely upon many, so that they feel as did the kindly old lady, "granny" Ross, of whom we have spoken, that they were "shut in " by so many people coming to the country. The census of the whole settlement in 1849 amounted to 5,291.

THE PARISHES.

No municipal government was ever provided for the people of Red River, though extensive petitions were forwarded to Britain for changes to be made in the government of the country. The Assiniboia council, however, passed certain ordinances, appointed road overseers, and from a slight tariff of four per cent. on imports, enough was raised to carry on public affairs. The local sub-divisions of Assiniboia were national and religious. French and Roman Catholics taking up a certain portion of river bank, Church of England half-breeds another, Scottish settlers and Presbyterians another. This was done sometimes by the will of the Hudson's Bay Company and sometimes without it. The first parish was Kildonan, so set apart and named by Lord Selkirk, on his visit in 1817 ; the De Meuron and Swiss settlement (1817-20) on the Seine, was the next, resulting in the parish of St. Boniface.

It was to this community with its varied elements and many conflicting interests that John Black found his way. It was here his life was spent, and with this people we shall see he at length threw in his lot. The population when he reached Red River was estimated at about 5,500 in all. The settlement was at length swallowed up in the Manitoba of to-day. It did its work though what that was will probably never be quite appreciated by those who see the Manitoba of to-day.

It marked the slow but sure process of an influence of the christianization and semi-civilization of many of our Indians; it gave the introduction from a barbarous and wandering life to habits of order and settled work ; it furnished a valuable pioneering and trading agency for the fur trade, for surveying our plains, and for our Canadian exploration. It gave the nucleus of the present educational and religious organizations, it made the Hudson's Bay Company not only a trading company but a company helping forward in different ways, the improvement of the Indians, and made them the friends of education and religion, and if we read the story of its history aright, it saved to Britain and Canada, the vast northwest which would otherwise not unlikely have met the fate of Oregon. And to do so great a work was not to fail.

CHAPTER VI.

Sowing and Weeping.

It was not strange that the mixture of population should be a matter of anxiety to the young pioneer of the Red River. Almost all the Highlanders and their descendants followed the newly-arrived preacher; but the Orkneymen, who had largely in the Hudson's Bay Company outposts married Indian women, seemed to form a guild of their own, and were more inclined to adhere to the Church of England. No doubt the Highland pride of character and connection of the Selkirk settlers kept the Orcadians at arm's length. Twenty years afterward the writer found a sentiment of this kind in Kildonan. The hope of Dr. Burns that John Black might, on account of his knowledge of French, gain an entrance to the Metis was never to any extent realized. Though never able to speak more than a few words of Indian, yet the minister had, as we shall afterwards see, a warm side for the red men.

Thus shut in, the young man found himself surrounded from the first by stalwart theologians, and for these he framed his habits of thought and course of action. So successfully did he do this that he reached their ideal as a preacher, though he knew not a word of Gaèlic, and "bore his faculties so meek" that he won unusual admiration and regard on Red River.

NO INFANCY OR CHILDHOOD.

The work of the hardy pioneer is usually a slow and painful process of gathering together a few people at a time, of making the community familiar with his voice and thought, and at last from a small beginning growing gradually stronger and stronger. This is the natural course of development, but in Kildonan Mr. Black found a congregation ready made, and it arose like Minerva, fully armed and scarcely needing equipment. Its infancy, childhood, and youth were all omitted. Within two months of Mr. Black's arrival, and while the people worshipped in the manse, which was used as a temporary church, the organization was begun.

At this time the pioneer wrote as follows :

" Red River, Dec. 17th, 1851.

" The temporary church will accommodate 250 or 300 persons, and is always well filled with a most attentive auditory. We have service forenoon and afternoon, and also a lecture on Wednesday. We have a large and interesting Sabbath-school. There are ninety-six scholars, thirty-six of whom are young people in my own class. Finding, as I did, that the congregation was pretty ripe for organization, I proceeded, with the help of a few of the heads of families, whom the people at my request appointed to aid me in the work, to examine and admit to the privilege of Church membership, such as presented themselves with this desire."

5

THE ELDERS OF THE PEOPLE.

In any other than a Highland community it would have been a dangerous experiment to choose elders so soon in the history of the congregation. But the Highlander has the natural tendency to follow leaders. His chief is everything to him. Every Highland community, by a process of natural selection—character of a lofty kind being a chief element—chooses its ideal men.

Precisely seven weeks after the first Presbyterian service was held in Red River six elders were chosen by ballot by the people who had been admitted by Mr. Black. Alexander Ross, of whom it was said that his work for the people for twenty-five years laid the people under a debt that they could never discharge, was chosen as leading elder. He died four years afterward. A second, James Fraser, a man of high spiritual power, filled the office for eleven years, till his death. George Munro, Donald Matheson, and John Sutherland made up the five who accepted office. One chosen, Robert McBeth, did not see his way to enter upon the office. The ordination of this first kirk session took place on the 7th of December. The young minister was always a wholesome upholder of the principle of doing everything "decently and in order." He did not even perform a baptism till the session was formed. A most interesting entry is made at this time in the session record : "On the same day as the ordination of the elders took place, the ordinance of baptism was dispensed for the first time in the congregation, the recipient being the child of Mr. Richard Salter, the only Englishman in the community. It was also the first baptism dispensed by the minister." At this time, too, came the recognition of the new minister by the governor and council of Assiniboia. A resolution was

passed authorizing any legally ordained Presbyterian minister belonging to the settlement to solemnize marriages.
This was regarded as a very considerable concession at the
time.

A HIGHLAND COMMUNION.

To the Highland imagination the communion stands out
as the great feast day at Jerusalem did to the ancient Jew.
The Celt is highly imaginative and is especially fervid.
Few of us can estimate how much religion owes in the old
world and the new to Celtic fervor. The communion is
looked forward to as an especially close approach to God
himself. At times we have to deplore a false view that
keeps some in Highland communities from coming forward until late in life to the Lord's table. How much it
must have meant to the exiles on Red River, forty years
after some of them had partaken of the communion in the
Kildonan in Sutherlandshire to now take part in Kildonan
on Red River.

Due preparation was made for the first celebration of
the New Testament feast by the newly constituted session.
On December 13th, 1851, the people met together for a
preparatory service—not now with perhaps thousands gathered from parishes far and near, but with the few hundreds
dwelling side by side. Tokens of admission to the Lord's
table were cautiously distributed, and we learn that the
position of the tables was carefully determined, as well as
the number of table services and the part each elder should
take in the administration. The method seen by the
writer twenty years after this date was then introduced. It
was to have the table covered with linen and to have it
successively occupied by different relays of communicants.
The number of communicants, at this first communion

after the Presbyterian form on Red River, was 45. The services following the communion were carried out as rigidly as those preceding it. Rev. John Black wrote in his description of this same service: " It was to all of us a solemn day, being the first time in which, according to our simple and scriptural form, that blessed ordinance was ever dispensed here. It was also the first time for the pastor who administered ; the first time for the elders who served ; and the first time for not a few who sat at the table—among others, two old men—the one 87 and the other 99 years of age ; and all this in addition to its own intrinsic solemnity."

ARISE AND BUILD !

To the settlers on Red River the only true ideal was that of the parish church—and it was the parish church of the beginning of this century when in the Highlands dissent was unknown. New settlers elsewhere have been willing to erect such temporary structures as their circumstances permit and to wait for better days. In new countries this plan has some advantages. But to the Highland hearts on Red River old Kildonan parish church must be reproduced in the Kildonan of the New World. But stone and mortar were needed, and there were few stone buildings in the settlement. The site on which the church was to be built had been given by the Hudson's Bay Company along with £150 toward the new church, as an equivalent to the people for their rights in St. John's Church which they relinquished to the Church of England, although they retained an interest in the burying ground in which their dead were lying. The new site at Frog Plain was really more centrally situated than that at St. John's for the Scottish settlers, and it contained glebe land amounting to some three hundred acres. Already their manse and school had been erected upon it. It had formerly been a camping place for the Indians, and of it Mr. Black remarked in one of his letters: "The church is to be erected on a piece of land long desecrated by the idolatrous revels of the Indians, and the Sabbath evening sports of some who bore a better name, but whose works were not so much better than theirs." Ten miles away from Red River on the open plain is an old Silurian outlier of limestone rock, which still furnishes building stone for Winnipeg. Even by the end of December the people had quarried at Stony Mountain nearly all the stone required, and with Red River cart or ox-sled had brought the most of the material to the new site on Frog Plain. The limestone of Stony Mountain produces excellent lime, and a sufficient quantity had already been burnt and placed on the ground ready for work in the spring. It was a time of earnest enthusiasm in Kildonan, and the most real parallel to it which comes to the mind of the writer is where in the days of Ezra after the captivity "the people gathered themselves together as one man to Jerusalem" and "when the builders laid the foundation of the temple of the Lord."

THE FLOODS OPPOSE.

The people but awaited the opening of spring in 1852 to erect the building for which they had the material on the ground. The winter had been one of great blessing to the newly-founded church. There had, however, been a great fall of snow and the swamps and streams had been filled with water in the autumn. The Red and Assiniboine rivers run through flat prairie lands, and an overflow in time of high water is very possible. In 1826 the valley of the Red River had been flooded, the water reaching in a great lake for miles across the country. The fathers of Kildonan remembered that former date when in 130 tents they had dwelt on Stony Mountain and the higher lands back from the river. Now to the people ardent to go on with their church building—which was all in all to their Highland hearts—it came as a great disappointment to see another flood, which, while not so great as the former, yet was very serious. We are fortunate in having a letter of Mr. Black's which gives us a vivid description of the

SCATTERING OF THE PEOPLE.

"Red River, May 27th, 1852.

"The only thing of great consequence of which I have to tell is that we are at present suffering from a great inundation—second only to that of the year 1826, of which you have heard. The consequence is that we are living in a tent on the Stony Hill, whither many have fled for shelter, and where I have been for more than two weeks and have the prospect of being so for some time longer.

"The ice began to break up on the river about the 23rd of April; by the 29th, the water was coming over the lower lands. Its increase was about a foot per day, and those whose houses were low had to flee to the heights on the 1st of May. Still rising, on the 7th and 8th the river began to carry down floating houses from the upper or French part of the settlement, where the banks are lower and the houses less substantial. On Sabbath 9th, I preached for the last time in our temporary church and had to go part of the way to it in a canoe. On Monday 10th, the flight from the Scotch part of the settlement was general. On that very day twenty-six years before had the poor people fled from the former flood.

" Such a scene it has never before been my lot to see. The water was now a considerable depth in many of the houses and flowing in behind them completely surrounded the people. In trying to reach a place of safety men and women were seen plunging through the water, driving and carrying, while the aged and little children were conveyed in carts drawn by oxen or horses. Most of the Scotch settlers had from 100 to 300 bushels of wheat in lofts which they kept from year to year in case of failure, and now for this there was much anxiety. The first night we encamped on the plain without wood or shelter, saving what we erected ; and amid the lowing of cattle and the bleating of sheep, and the roaring of calves, and the squealing of pigs, and the greeting of bairns, you may be sure we had a concert. After three days we arrived here which is a beautiful woody ridge far from water mark, but thirteen miles from our houses. A few families are with me here, but my congregation is scattered, so that, from extreme to extreme is, I suppose, more than thirty miles

A SEA OF WATERS.

" Thus the waters prevailed and spread themselves over the cultivated lands, sweeping away everything loose and much that was thought fast. Houses, barns, byres, stacks of wheat, etc., were floating down thick and fast. The rail fences—and there were no other—were swept clean away. Not a bridge is left on the road in all the flooded district. Sometimes the wind blew very strong, and acting on the lakelike expanse of waters agitated them like a sea, and this was very destructive to the houses of the settlers. The breadth flooded in our part of the settlement might be eight or nine miles, while the ordinary width of the river is not more than 150 yards. The destruction of property has been immense. From 3,000 to 4,000 people have been driven from their homes, though the water did not rise so high as in 1826 by 3 feet 6 inches. I have crossed this wide expanse twice to visit our people on the east side. It is like a great lake. I have now three preaching stations instead of one—*all camp meetings.* The water began to fall about the 21st. We hope to be home again in about two weeks. Our sacrament was to have been held last Sabbath, but we have had to defer it indefinitely. The whole will be a serious blow to the settlement, and will be an injury to the congregation. Many will be rendered much less able to pay their subscriptions for church building."

HOME AGAIN.

The pastor and his people reached their desolated homes in June. The country presented a dreary aspect. Crops to a limited extent were sown and yet the harvest, though the floods had done their worst, according to the promise did not fail. The church building was again taken up. The flood during its continuance had destroyed a considerable portion of the lime prepared for the building. A quantity of lumber was drifted off, and timbers for the couples had been floated away but were secured again. The people resumed the work with great cheerfulness. During the season following, the church was erected. Alexander Ross in his "Red River Settlement," says: " It was finished in 1853 ; and though small, it is considered the neatest and most complete church in the colony. It is seated for 510 persons and is always well filled. Its cost was £1,050 stg. The manse is also completed ; and it is pleasing to add that when it was finished there was not a shilling due on either church or manse."

In 1853 Mr. Black returned to Canada, and spent the summer there. He was induced to return to Red River,

KILDONAN PARISH CHURCH.

and had the pleasure of opening the new church in January, 1854.   His heart was gladdened.

" He that goeth forth and weepeth, bearing precious seed, shall doubtless come again with rejoicing, bringing his sheaves with him."

CHAPTER VII

Pastor and Parish.

The uncertainty as to whether he was to be the permanent leader of the Red River Presbyterians remained for years in · the mind of John Black. Five years at least after his arrival we find him wondering whether the committee intended to recall him or not. This arose from a strain in his nature which rendered him liable to depression, and also from a deep desire to see the spiritual development of the people, which he determined should not be hindered by his personal defects. He was a man of intense humility. In the year after the Red River flood (1853), when he saw the church building fairly under way, he returned to Canada, undoubtedly to allow a substitute to be sent if such were possible. The impression made by the pioneer missionary during his year and a half of labor had been so marked that the people of Red River were determined that he should not be replaced.

The Hudson's Bay Company, as before stated, had been averse to another denomination entering Rupert's Land until they saw that the Presbyterians could not be refused. Then Sir George Simpson, with a stroke of diplomacy,

allowed the privilege in his letter to Rev. Mr. Rintoul, of
·Montreal.   The company's attitude was still for various reasons one of caution.   Mr. Black had been exceedingly
wise and politic.   In one of his letters he states that at
times when his inclination had impelled him to interfere
yet he had studiously refrained from taking sides in the
struggle which was beginning between the company and
the people.   He had a strong sense of the fact that he was
an ambassador of peace.   That he had succeeded well is
shown by an extract from a letter written him by Sheriff
Ross on his first return to Toronto.

SIR GEORGE SIMPSON WON OVER.

" Colony Gardens, Red River, June 29th, 1853.

" I have just had an interview with Sir George Simpson,
the Governor-in-Chief of Rupert's Land, who regrets very
much he had not been in time to see you before you left
the settlement, and desires me to write immediately and
intimate to you, that he would be most happy to see you in
passing through Toronto.

" Sir George has expressed himself in a very kind and
friendly manner, and says that from the high sense the
committee in London entertains of your moderation, zeal,
and peace-working ministrations, while in the colony, he is
authorized to convey to you a sense of its esteem
for your character and to grant you a certain sum annually
from the company as minister of the Presbyterian congregation in Red River, and adds, ' If I had been here I should
not have consented to Mr. Black's leaving the settlement at
this time.'

" In connection with what has been said, I must further
observe that the offer Sir George is prepared to make to

you, on the part of the company as already stated is not to
be considered to be made to any Presbyterian clergyman
that may come to labor in Red River, no, *but to you*, dis-
tinctly intended for you, for the great satisfaction you have
given and the high esteem you are held in by all classes in
the colony. This high and flattering opinion of the company at home will, we trust, be an additional motive for
your return to resume your duties among us. We all look
for it, will expect it, if God spare your health."

THE PIONEER RETURNS.

After an absence of five months the longed for pastor
returned. The committee had not succeeded in finding
one to replace him, and, indeed, do not seem to have striven
hard to do so. In a spirit of submission he turned north-
westward, though immediately on his arrival he wrote to his
aged father: "Whether the Canadian Church will allow
me to stay here or not I do not yet know. I am perfectly
willing to return if they get some one to supply the place.
For some reasons I would wish it to be so. We shall see."
His return to Red River on this occasion was one that even
he confessed to be "tedious and toilsome." He actually
took forty-nine days to reach his destination, starting from
Galena, on the Mississippi river. On his northward journey
he reached the establishment of the Presbyterian missionaries at Red Lake, in Minnesota. Supplied by these kind
friends with pemican, bread, and flour, Mr. Black and his
voyageur, about the end of October, pushed through Red
Lake in their birch bark canoe, the missionary having to
paddle as well as the boatman. On the third day, on account of the ice, the canoe could proceed no further. Un-
willingly the travellers retraced their course and reached

again the shelter of their missionary friends. In the following week the start was again made, but again to be interrupted by ice. The party then camped on the shore for several days, until the ice would bear their weight, when they proceeded on their slippery way. They walked over the ice for forty miles, until having obtained a horse and cart they reached by land carriage, in four and a half days, Pembina, a fort on the boundary line.

At the Pembina trading post a good Presbyterian fur trader named Murray supplied the pioneers with a conveyance, and the journey was again resumed to Fort Garry. The horse was weak and the weather cold, and so Mr. Black trudged most of the way and reached the Ross mansion, near Fort Garry, at the close of his last day's walk of forty miles. Surely it needs a man of iron frame for frontier mission work ! And yet Mr. Black writes of this journey with a cheerful heart: "During all these hardships and toils and disappointments, sleeping in the open air in northern frosts, I have reason to bless God I have enjoyed the most vigorous health and have not as much as caught a cold."

THE CURE OF SOULS.

With the new Church now almost ready the pastor settled down to regular work. His parish proper was his kingdom. He regarded every parishioner as worthy of his attention and most anxious thought. Years after it was a well-known sight to behold the faithful pastor, staff in hand, a gray checked plaid thrown over one shoulder, and with light moccasined feet tripping along the banks of Red River on his errand of mercy. On account of the settlement of Red River, being like that of the French Canadians along the

St. Lawrence, his parish was an example of length without breadth. The Kildonan houses were in two rows, facing each other from each side of the river, and made a continuous village along each bank. The writer has heard the announcement from Kildonan pulpit that the pastor, during the coming week, would visit from the house of Mr. Donald Matheson to that of Mr. Samuel Matheson. On another occasion from Mr. Harper's to Mr. Gunn's, and the like. These visits were very thorough. All the children expected the minister; all the housewives had their houses swept and garnished; even the men, on the day of the expected visit, laid aside their working garb, and the godly pastor emulated, in many ways, Goldsmith's "village preacher." As everyone knows, every preacher has not the faculty of successful visitation of the sick. This was, however, an especially strong feature of the Kildonan pastor. His sympathy, deep feeling, and wise regard for the condition of the invalid, are spoken of to this day. In cases of severe illness his visits were daily and unremitting.

" In his duty prompt at every call
He watched, wept, prayed, and felt for all."

THE PARISH SCHOOL.

To a man brought up in the parish schools of his native land, and so impressed with the value of education, the parish school of Scotland was the model. The conditions in Red River settlement were favorable for it. John Knox's ideal of the parish church and manse and parish school were easily realizable; and so church and school went up side by side. Even before the church was built we find the following entry (1852) in a letter by the pioneer: "The York Factory boats have just come and brought the annual supply of goods. They have brought in the box of school books which we had ordered all safe. We have, among other things, ten large wall maps. Our school will now be the best furnished in the settlement."

The Kildonan parish school always retained its pre-eminence on the Red River. The government of the country under the Hudson's Bay Company gave no aid. The Church of England and Catholics had their schools supported by private effort, and the Kildonan parish school was of the same kind. Even after the transfer of the Red River country to Canada the writer remembers being present at a Kildonan school meeting when it was decided still to continue the support of the school by voluntary subscriptions. Mr. Black was soon instrumental in sending three Kildonan young men to Toronto to complete their education. Donald Fraser, a youth of great promise, who died early; Alex. Matheson, afterwards a minister of the Church, and now a resident of his native parish of Kildonan; and James Ross, son of Sheriff Ross, a young man who was afterwards on the editorial staff of the Toronto *Globe*. The pastor afterwards at times helped studious boys privately with their Latin and Greek, and did his best to encourage good education in the parish.

THE PREACHER.

But great as John Black was as a pastor and as an educator, he was not less noted as a preacher. He always retained the dialect of the Scottish south country, but this was modified somewhat by a pronunciation, said to have arisen from his use of French in his mission work. He pronounced the letter *a* broad in such words as "grace," "congregation," and the like. His manner was very free

and natural, though in voice he was possibly a little louder
than some would have desired. He was, however, regarded
all over the country as an excellent preacher. The writer
remembers his first opportunity of hearing John Black, and
this more than a quarter of a century ago. Kildonan
Church was plain, even to severity. On the right hand, as
you entered the church, was a small vestry under the stair-
Here the pastor entered, and waited for the signal from the
ringing bell, as it called the worshippers from all parts of
the parish. It was the custom always to use the Geneva
gown. On the morning referred to, Mr. Black came forth,
gowned, as the bell ceased, and ascended the high pulpit.
In accordance with the custom of the country at that time,
the pastor was shod with moccasins, which gave the quick,
lively motion which so characterized him. The psalm was
given out with rapid movement and much impressiveness,
the prayer was purely extempore, and entered with considerable minuteness into the needs of his people, and
marked a man of unmistakable devotion. The lessons were
read with perhaps a want of variety. When the preacher
began his sermon it was evident, from the attitude assumed
by his auditors, that they regarded this as the chief part of
the service, and that they waited with expectancy for its
development. Mr. Black always wrote his sermons in full,
and had the sermon before him in the pulpit. Like Dr.
Chalmers, however, he was not hampered by his "manu-
script." As the preacher opened his subject, it was plain
to see that his method was textual and expository, and
showed intimate acquaintance with Scripture. As the sermon progressed the speaker became more and more ani-
mated, and frequently rose to the heights of eloquence.
His denunciation of sin and wrong doing were fearless, and

6

at times reminded one of the fervor of the Hebrew pro-
phets. He was, however, very tender, and frequently was
moved to tears, and his appeals to sinners were most touching and effective. In Mr. Black's preaching there was much
variety of subject, though there was little of dealing with
popular questions of the day. Congregation and preacher
alike had very strict views as to what was dignified and
suitable to the house of God. As a result of the high
standard of preaching of the pioneer, the Kildonan people
became excellent judges of sermonizing, and after hearing
many preachers in the later part of Mr. Black's ministry
and since that time, are of opinion that Mr. Black was the
greatest of them all.

HABITS OF STUDY.

That Mr. Black was able to maintain himself in the same
congregation for thirty years as an interesting preacher
arose, no doubt, from his systematic method of study. In
writing during his earlier ministry to his brother, who was
also a minister, and had been settled in Caledonia, Upper
Canada, Mr. Black says : " How do you get along with
study? What is your plan in preparing sermons? Do
you write fully and commit, or how? What are your general studies? How many hours a day can you spend?
Tell me all about it—your Hebrew, Greek, philosophy,
theology, etc. How are you in natural science and astron-
omy, geology, etc.? These and such like branches we
would need to study nowadays if we would not be despised
by everyone with a smattering of knowledge. My much
travelling and my long separation from my books have
inflicted an injury upon me that I will never recover I suppose in this world. I am trying to study four hours a day

four days in the week—the other two are devoted to ser-
mon-making. My subjects are Greek Testament, Hebrew
Bible, systematic or philosophical theology, and practical
theology, and an hour to Biblical interpretation. Of course
I indulge to some extent also in general reading. The work
that has attracted my mind most of late in the theological
department is McCosh's ' Divine Government,' which I
esteem about the noblest performance that ever I read. I
lay out my time regularly, but am constantly getting into
debt and becoming a literary bankrupt, failing to carry out
my plans. And so I have almost given up hope of ever
being anything more than a third or fourth-rate man."

Such words as these show the aspiration of the true
student, and show Mr. Black to have been a man well qual-
ified to shine in the highest walks of Church and scholarly
life.

DOMESTIC LIFE.

On the return of Mr. Black from his first visit to Canada
the longing of his heart for domestic sympathy shewed
itself. Indeed it was a necessity of his life that he should
be surrounded by friends and companions. That he needed the cheering influence of friends was shown all through
his career. No one ever loved his friends more strongly,
delighted more to sit and spend hour after hour in a social
chat, and loved home life more tenderly than he. The
house of Sheriff Ross had been his home from the first day
of his arrival in Red River Settlement. It was not strange
that his heart should incline to Henrietta Ross, one of the
tall and handsome daughters found in the numerous family
of his Highland host. Miss Ross was, it is true, one of the
daughters of the land, being, as we have seen, on the

mother's side, related to the Okanagan Indians of the Rocky Mountains. This attachment created, indeed, a ripple of excitement among the Scottish settlers, who were somewhat exclusive in their notions, but Miss Ross was attractive in appearance, well educated, having had the advantages of the excellent " McCallum School " at St. John's, and was distinguished for Christian character and worth.

So the pastor was married and the establishment seemed to Mr. Black complete—church, school, manse, and the last now with the appearance and tone of home. In this home there grew to manhood and womanhood three sons and three daughters, all living to-day in different places in the valley of Red River. One of the family the pastor named after the father of the Red River Mission, Robert Burns. In the collection of letters is a most pathetic account of the death by accident of this promising little boy, and the sore bereavement seems to have for years cast a deep shadow over the Kildonan manse. The home thus found-ed was the very abode of hospitality. The circumstances of Red River were such that suitable accommodation for visitors or newcomers was very hard to obtain. The boun-tiful table at the manse was rarely without visitors, and the writer, a quarter of a century after enjoying such hospitali-ty, still remembers the kind-hearted and noble mistress of the manse. The home at Kildonan was plunged into the deepest gloom by the death of Mrs. Black in 1873. The day of the funeral is still remembered as one of the coldest and fiercest days of the cold years of the early seventies. It was long before the desolated hearts of the husband and children recovered from the terrible stroke. Dr. Black some years after married Miss Bannatyne, a lady connected with one of the leading families of the country. She was a mother indeed to the motherless children, and still lives in the family home in Kildonan.

PUBLIC DUTIES.

With a sympathy for every good work Mr. Black was identified with every moral movement in Red River Settlement. Coming as he did to people who had had for forty years an unfortunate religious experience, he had naturally to take a firm stand against evil of every kind. The Highland ideal of church discipline is very high, and Mr. Black seemed equally solicitous with his people to suppress aggravated forms of sin. It would neither be interesting nor expedient to detail the session cases which came up as the years rolled on. There was one thing always to be said, that the moderator never flinched in his duty, but it is plain to see that he rather aimed at the reclamation of the wrongdoer, than took satisfaction in meting out punishment to the offender. He associated himself very heartily with the ministers of the Church of England, who welcomed his assistance in joint meetings for prayer and temperance reform throughout the parishes. He was instrumental in carrying out the work of the Bible Society. He was also very anxious to gain the acquaintance of the officers and men of the Hudson's Bay Company—many of them his countrymen—scattered over the Northwest. With these men he kept up a correspondence, and hardly a chief factor or trader from the interior visited Fort Garry, who did not think it a duty and a pleasure to take the five miles journey from the Fort to Kildonan manse to visit the representative of the church of his fathers. So strong did this feeling become that in 1862 Governor Dallas invited Mr.

Black to hold service at Fort Garry, and this was undertaken with the approval of Kildonan session, and thus was
begun the first Presbyterian service on the site of the city
of Winnipeg, which has become one of the strongholds of
the Presbyterian Church in Canada to-day.   In every good
thing the Kildonan pastor was a leader, and while his sympathetic nature encouraged many a confidence, and many a
sad story that caused him trouble and anxiety, yet he was
full of resource, and thought nothing of pain and trouble
and expense if he might be helpful to the vicious, or lead
the young into wisdom's ways,

> " As a bird each fond endearment tries
> To tempt its new-fledg'd offspring to the skies,
> He tried each art, reprov'd each dull delay,
> Allur'd to brighter worlds, and led the way ! "

REV. JAMES NISBET,
Presbyterian Pioneer Indian Missionary, 1866.

CHAPTER VIII

A Kindred Spirit.

It might not be right to say that it was John Black's intermarriage with the native people of the country and the fact of his own children having Indian blood rather than the Christian sentiment in favor of carrying the Gospel to the wandering Indian tribes of the prairies, that more strongly influenced him, but it is certain that early in his ministry he began to cry out for a Presbyterian mission among the Indians. His ardent appeal led to the synod so early as 1857 passing a resolution in favor of undertaking this work. The comforting task of passing favorable resolutions was indulged in for ten years, but toward the end of this decade some money had been accumulated and the church undertook its first work among the Red Indians of the plains.

This period was a time of much anxiety to John Black, the ardent advocate of the project. Sitting in his lonely study on Red River it was discouraging to read letters from Toronto telling how one year more, and another year, and so on was deemed necessary to mature the scheme. One year he refers to the agitation going on at the Red River in

favor of union with Canada and to a petition signed by upwards of five hundred heads of families being forwarded
to the British government to further this object.   John
Black's chief thought was that if the petition were granted,
and the northwest became a part of Canada, something
would surely then be done for the poor Indian.

A SELECTION MADE.

While not quite prepared to undertake the mission the
church went so far in 1862 as to send to Mr. Black's assistance at Red River, one of its ministers who should be engaged in learning the Indian language, and otherwise preparing himself for the Indian work resolved on.   This
agent was Rev. James Nisbet, minister of Oakville, Upper
Canada.   James Nisbet was of a missionary family, his
brother, Dr. Nisbet, who paid a visit to Canada, more than
a quarter of a century ago, having been honored to take a
leading place in the South Sea mission of the Free Church
of Scotland.   James Nisbet had come out to Canada from
Scotland full of the fervor of the period of the disruption
and though a skillful tradesman, had thrown in his lot with
the first band of students which entered Knox College.
The minister of Kildonan and he had been fellow students
and co-workers, and now that James Nisbet had been appointed to Red River, John Black found in him a kindred
spirit.

On his arrival in 1862, being an unmarried man, he became a resident at the Kildonan Manse, and we find fre-
quent reference, in the collection of letters, to the hearty co-
operation of the two ministers, and the spirit of rejoicing
that now they could overtake Kildonan, Little Britain,
Headingly, and the new station to which the Governor had

given an invitation at Fort Garry. Mr. Nisbet while an
earnest preacher, and as Mr. Black writes, "working dili-
gently and acceptably," yet had a remarkable liking for
building. At Kildonan there is still pointed out the parish
schoolhouse, a stone building, much of the woodwork of
which was done by Mr. Nisbet personally. Mr. Nisbet
very readily fell into the ways of the Red River people, and
two or three years after his arrival was married to Mary
McBeth, a member of one of the best known Kildonan
families, and sister of the present minister of Augustine
Church, Winnipeg.

HEATHEN INDIANS.

The question of how and where to begin work among
the Indians was a difficult one, and on Mr. Black largely
fell the responsibility of determining the question. He
had the confidence of the committee in the east, and he
was the friend of the Hudson's Bay Company in the far
west. The Church of England and Roman Catholics were
carrying on work among the Swampy Crees, Saulteaux, and
other Ojibways about Lake of the Woods and Lake Manitoba, as well as in the far off Mackenzie River district,
while the former had almost a monopoly of the missions
around Hudson Bay. The English Wesleyans had for
years carried on missions among the Indians near Norway
House and the north end of Lake Winnipeg, and after the
visit of John Ryerson, whose letters about the region were
published, the work was taken over by the Methodist
Church in Canada. It was manifest that the call sent
the Presbyterian Church was to the Indians of the western
prairies, who had only seen the passing missionary and
were still in absolute heathenism. After much deliberation

it was decided to undertake work among the Crees of the plains, of whom there were said to be from ten to fifteen thousand largely without the gospel.

These Indians are among the finest physically and mentally of the Canadian Indians. They are of the same race as the Ojibways, belonging to the great Algonquin family known on the Atlantic sea-board and continuing along the Laurentian country to the north of our Canadian lake chain. Leaving behind the rocky regions where the birchbark canoe and wigwam, and the fish of the streams, with the game of the forest, had been their chief dependence, the Crees of the Plains used horses, of which they had numerous bands, chased the buffalo to obtain a bountiful subsistence, and lived in leathern teepees. The language of the Crees, while the same in structure as that of the Ojibways, has yet its vocabulary much modified from that of the parent tongue. While the Crees, in their love of the buffalo and fondness for following the herds over the plains, were thoroughly nomadic and likely to be difficult to evangelize, yet the task was undertaken cheerfully. Their great camps were the scenes of the wildest excitement and greatest excesses, and yet they were a brave, self-reliant, and able people. The cut given of four of their chiefs who visited Brantford at the time of the unveiling of the Brant statue in 1886, gives a good illustration of the appearance of staidness and solidity found among them.

THE TASK BEGUN.

In 1865 Mr. Nisbet was recommended to the synod for a mission among this uncivilized but interesting people. The gravity of the enterprise is to be borne in mind. Hudson's Bay Company traders had for many years ventured among the tribes of the plains. The Hudson's Bay Company trader, however, had the Union Jack flying over him ; he was housed in a strong fort ; in his hands were weapons, and the power of the company was felt over the whole land ; but the missionary came with a message of peace ; he had no emblem of force about him, he preached the doctrine, "If one cheek was smitten to turn the other also," and so to proceed 500 miles from Red River and break ground on the Saskatchewan, to be largely dependent on the locality for sustenance, and to trust to the good-will of the Indians, required courage and resource. And these qualities James Nisbet had. He was not a man of display, was a man of quiet, undemonstrative manner, but had no cowardice or surrender in him. Like his countryman, the Highland piper, who was asked to play the "retreat," he could reply that he had never learned that tune. Mr. Nisbet's theology was of a very exact kind. He was in the habit of advising complete reliance in God, perhaps there was a strain of the severe, even of the stoical, in it ; but in the case of our pioneer Indian missionary, he lived out and exemplified it as well as preached it.

FOR CHRIST AND COUNTRY.

A journey from the Red River to the Saskatchewan by the Canadian Pacific Railway to-day is a comparatively trifling matter, taking twenty-five or thirty hours ; but thirty years ago it meant much. It required an outfit that could serve the purpose for forty or fifty days. The sending of a missionary, known to the people of Kildonan and by marriage one of themselves, profoundly stirred the Highland parish. In one of Mr. Black's letters he states that the people of the parish had raised between £80 and £100 sterling for the purpose of making a suitable send-off for the man who had become so popular among them.

Mr. Nisbet's plan, in so far as we can gather, was from the first to be practical and industrial. His effort was to induce the nomadic Indians to settle, to cultivate the land, and to make the Indian independent of the precarious results of the chase. In order to accomplish his ideal it was necessary to provide himself with a considerable establishment, so that the mission party, inclusive of his wife and little child and two other children, numbered ten persons. They were provided with the necessary outfit for hunting, fishing, building, and farming. The day of departure was the 6th of June, 1866, and it was a day of great moment for Kildonan. The Saskatchewan was being looked to as the land of promise. Gold had been discovered in its sands, and one of Mr. Black's letters mentions that a number of Kildonan young men had been among the fortunate explorers. The establishment had about it the air of a Kildonan enterprise, and these elements added wider interest to the Christian effort to evangelize the heathen, which was so dear to Mr. Nisbet's heart. It was a high day for John Black, for he had felt it a scandal that his church should be the only one of the four churches at work in Rupert's Land not doing something for the aborigines of the country.

INTO THE WILDERNESS.

We are fortunate in having a letter, quoted in Dr. Gregg's " Short History," giving in Mr. Nisbet's own words an account of the journey into the wilderness. From this we make a few extracts :

" All our goods were carried in carts ; each cart was drawn by one ox, harnessed something like a horse. Mrs. Nisbet and our little girl and a young woman rode on a light wagon with a canvas top, such as you sometimes use in Canada. For myself I was generally on horseback but frequently walking, as the oxen do not go very fast. We had tents, such as soldiers use, which we pitched every night, and in them we were generally very comfortable. The Sabbaths were delightful to us. Both men and animals were prepared for the weekly rest. It was pleasant to see the poor oxen evidently enjoying the rich pasture of the wilderness and the rest they had from their daily toil. We had regular Sabbath services, and they were very devout.

" We had a good many creeks and rivers to cross, and I dare say you would have been much amused had you seen the plans that were fallen upon for crossing such as were too deep for loaded carts. Few of my friends in the east have seen a boat made with two cartwheels tied together and an oilcloth spread over them, or one made of ox hides sewed together and stretched on a rough frame, that would take two carts and their loads at a time. Such were the contrivances for getting over streams where there are no bridges or large boats by which we could cross. We passed over a great deal of beautiful country, with hills and valleys, streams, lakes, and ponds. Hundreds of ducks were swimming about in the little lakes, and sometimes they furnished dinners for us. Sandhill cranes were also seen occasionally, and a few of them were shot for our Sabbath dinners. Forty days after we left our Red River homes we got to a place called Carlton House, on the north branch of the great Saskatchewan River, and there we camped for one week, while I went to see some places that I could fix upon for our future home."

PRINCE ALBERT FOUNDED.

At Carlton, George Flett, the interpreter of the mission, who had been in the service of the Hudson's Bay Company at Edmonton, met the party. He has since become known to the Church as its oldest living Indian missionary. Born on the Saskatchewan of Scottish and Indian extraction, he had received a good English education at the schools on Red River. His wife was a member of the Ross family, being a sister of Mrs. John Black. The gathering of missionary agents also included Mr. John McKay, a Scoto-French-Indian native, who belonged to a family well known at Red River for its energy and influence. John McKay was married to a sister of Mrs. Nisbet, and he steadfastly clung to Mr. Nisbet in the prosecution of the Indian work.

The party at Fort Carlton made a considerable impression upon the Indians. While the Indians were glad to see so many of the Red River people coming to them, yet some trouble arose when the decision was made to settle at a point sixty miles south-east of Carlton House and not far from the forks where the north and south branches of the Saskatchewan unite. No treaties had as yet been made with the Indians, and they objected to the incomers erecting buildings, ploughing fields, and taking possession of the land as the agents of the mission proposed to do. George Flett was the useful man for the occasion. His mother's people were Crees, and he was among the very band, whose members he recognized as relations. With his characteristic shrewdness he claimed his portion and gave permission to the Red River party to utilize his rights. This claim seems to have been at once admitted by the Cree band of the locality. The new mission was appropriately named after the Prince Consort, Albert the Good, who had passed away a few years before.

MISSION WORK BEGUN.

The plan of the establishment was soon vigorously worked out. During the first year two small buildings were erected, and what was since known as the large mission building in the year after. A school was immediately opened, a farm begun, and every means taken to attract the Indians to the place. As was not unnatural, the maimed, the halt, and the blind were brought to the kind-hearted missionary, aud it must be stated that no small trouble was experienced in protecting the missionary from the cunning and the lazy among the Indian bands. The Indian's view of salvation is very often a willingness to accept the white man's religion provided the consideration offered is sufficient. How to meet this difficulty was one of Mr. Nisbet's chief concerns.

For four years Mr. Black was the sole intermediary between the Foreign Mission Committee of the Church and Mr. Nisbet. When the Presbytery of Manitoba was established in 1870 matters took a slightly different shape. A Foreign Mission Committee of Presbytery was formed, of which Mr. Black was convenr

Mr. Nisbet did such itinerant work as he was able. He journeyed to Edmonton, a point upwards of 400 miles west of Prince Albert. He visited the Indians of Carlton House once a month and had success with them. But the management of an industrial centre, such as Prince Albert had become, was plainly inconsistent with any large amount of sowing the Gospel "broadcast" among the wandering tribes, from fifty to five hundred miles away.   Another difficulty overtook Prince Albert as an Indian mission in a few years after its founding.   It was the centre of a fertile region very attractive to white settlers.   The white settlement led the bands of wandering Crees to retreat to more remote districts.   The writer in 1871 became a member of the Presbytery's Committee, of which Mr. Black was convener, and well remembers the unrest of the period.

At this time the large expense of an establishment like Prince Albert was meeting opposition in the Church and this, along with the other considerations stated, brought much trouble to the venerable convener in regard to the mission which he loved as a child of his own.   In 1872 Dr. Moore, of Ottawa, went as a delegate to the Saskatchewan, in behalf of the General Assembly.   His report led to the discontinuance of the industrial phase of the mission, but it also rendered a tribute of commendation and praise to the faithful work that had been done by the founder, to the high reputation borne by the mission among all the bands of Crees, and to the steady influence for righteousness attached to the name of James Nisbet.   In the course of time the Indian mission at Prince Albert ceased to be, unless the mission school among a wandering band of Sioux still maintained there be so regarded.   John McKay, afterwards ordained, was invited to a band of Crees north of Carlton, and till his death ministered to Mistawasis' band.   Other churches have taken hold of the bands about Prince Albert, and to-day as a result direct or indirect, of James Nisbet's work, few Indians of the district are without he Gospel.

Shortly after Dr. Moore's visit to Prince Albert, Mr. Nis-

bet and his wife visited his old home in Ontario, and he
was present at the General Assembly of 1873. He returned
to his dear Prince Albert, but being left alone by the resig-
nation of Rev. Edward Vincent who had come to Manitoba, and findinghis plans somewhat changed by the action
of the Church, he arrived with his wife at Kildonan, in
September, seeking a temporary rest. The writer well
remembers them as they returned. Their work seemed to
be done, and the Presbytery soon decided to lay hands on
Hugh McKellar, an earnest student, and license and ordain
him for the work in Prince Albert. Mrs. Nisbet soon
passed away in the home where she was born, and eleven
days afterward her husband followed her. They are together
in Kildonan churchyard. His grave marks the spot where
lies as true, brave and single-minded a man as ever laid a
foundation stone in the work of missions.

A NEW DEPARTURE.

Though Mr. Black as Convener of the Foreign Mission
Committee of the Presbytery had some sympathy for the
industrial ideal of Missions among the Indians held by Mr.
Nisbet, yet, on the decision of the General Assembly being
given, he loyally accepted the plan proposed, of attending
simply to evangelistic work among the tribes and to teaching the young. It is to be remembered, however, that
between 1866 and 1874 circumstances had changed. It
was evident in 1874 that the buffalo was soon to be a thing
of the past, and the Canadian Government approved the
plan of settling the Indians upon reserves and of teaching
them to be farmers. The policy of the Government thus
left the Church to pursue its own method.

The Committee now began to extend its work. George

7

Flett, who had left Prince Albert Mission in 1869, was sent to two bands, one near Fort Pelly, the other on the west side of Riding Mountain. These missions were very successful. Mr. Flett was ordained as an Indian missionary, and lived to see the Okanese Reserve on Little Saskatchewan entirely Christianized. The Fort Pelly band was left to a young half-breed of Red River, Cuthbert McKay, since dead, and has grown to be the Crowstand Mission of to-day. In 1875 the Sioux or Dakota band of refugees from the United States living on the Birdtail Creek were taken under the care of the Presbytery's Foreign Mission Committee and a pure blooded Sioux missionary from the States obtained for them. This mission is still maintained, and is part of the constituency of the Birtle Indian boarding school.

Mr. Black lived long enough to see the Mistawasis, Okanese, Pelly, and Birdtail missions fairly established. Nothing delighted him more than to preside at the meeting of his committee, read the letters from the missionaries, and then to write the necessary letters of counsel and advice, and at times even of gentle fault-finding, which were agreed on. All his friends lament that he passed away too soon to know of Round Lake, File Hills, the western Qu'Appelle Valley reserves and the Portage la Prairie, Birtle and Regina Indian schools. He saw enough, however, to assure him that his dream of a Christianized Indian population would in the end be realized.

CHAPTER IX

Red River Becomes Canadian.

The union of Red River Settlement with Canada was in the air in 1857. In a letter to his brother, Mr. Black, after discussing the reasons given by the settlers for the change, says in his own cautious way : "I do not know whether Canadian annexation will much better them. However, it looks as if the time was come for a change, and if we suffer some inconvenience during the transition period perhaps 'the good time coming' may compensate for all. I have taken no part for or against the movement. I do not think it is good for ministers to jump into the maelstrom of politics. Let them stop till they are pushed in. I have my views and preferences, *and aiblins it wadna hae taen a muckle dunch to ding me in*, but in the meantime I am better pleased to be out."

While Mr. Black was thus so politic the leaders among the people of Red River were by no means undecided. The movement seems to have taken so strong a form that the greater part of the people, who were not immediately connected with the Hudson's Bay Company, strongly favored it.

Ten or eleven years before this, the desire for self-government took a much more disagreeable form. Petitions from some of the people of Red River at that time were to the American Government asking it to "annex the Red River Territory to the United States, and promising assistance against the Hudson's Bay Company in case of war."

BUT WE SHALL BE FREE.

This shameful proposal had completely failed, but now a large petition to "The President of the Executive Council, Toronto, Canada," was signed by "Roderick Kennedy and 574 others," reciting their grievances, and appealing for reception by Canada. The petition says : " We love the British Name ! we are proud of that glorious fabric, the British Constitution, raised by the wisdom, cemented and hallowed by the blood of our forefathers. . . . It will be seen, therefore, that we have no other choice than the Canadian plough and printing press, or the American rifle and fugitive slave law."

One of the most active and influential men in this movement was the Hon. David Gunn, the leading elder in the Little Britain congregation. A Caithness Highlander, he had come out in Lord Selkirk's time, had been schoolmaster, meteorological observer, Smithsonian agent, and now took a leading part in all public matters. Being the literary man of the movement, he wrote a document setting forth very well the advantages of the Red River country, and showing the profit the country would be to Canada. This statement may be found in the government publications of the time. Donald Gunn lived for many years after and became a member of the Legislative Council of Manitoba after Confederation.

Canada made a strong effort under the leadership of Chief Justice Draper and others to obtain the Northwest, and the British Commons ordered a complete investigation by committee into the case, but it took a number of years more to bring about the desired result.

CANADIAN SETTLERS.

Immediately after this movement, Canadian settlers began to drop by ones and twos into the Red River Settlement. An important exploration of the Red River, Assiniboine, and Saskatchewan Valleys took place by Henry Youle Hind, and the report of this was at the time a mine of interesting and useful information. The well-known Dr. Schultz arrived in 1859. Two English-Canadians, Messrs. Buckingham and Coldwell, came to the settlement at this time with a printing press, and began to publish the *Nor'-Wester*, the first newspaper of the country. This paper soon passed into other hands, and had a stormy existence, being regarded by many, ceitainly by the Hudson's Bay Company, as a disturber of the peace. The arrival of a number of aggressive and determined men during this decade introduced much strife into the hitherto quiet and easy-going settlement, and the weakness of the Hudson's Bay Company, which was rather uncertain of its powers, encouraged restless spirits to insubordination. The formation of what was called a "Canadian party" during this time certainly did not improve the chances of a peaceful and speedy union of the country with Canada. Shortly after the transfer the writer remembers Mr. Black when speaking of the disturbed and clamorous times through which we were passing, sighing for "the peaceful days of the old Red River." Oh! but responded the writer, in his

youthful Canadian enthusiasm, "Surely you would not
have the broad acres of Red River locked up from cultiva-
tion ! Life is hardly worth living without progress !"
" Better fifty years of Europe than a cycle in Cathay."
" Well, perhaps so," said Mr. Black, "but there are
animals that like to lie at the bottom of the pool and bask
in peace and quiet."

THE GRASSHOPPERS.

The steady flow of small groups of Canadians to the
banks of the Red and Assiniboine rivers, and the interest
taken by a few of the representatives in the Canadian Parliament led to negotiations of a more definite kind between
the Canadian government, the Imperial government and
the Hudson's Bay Company.   In the year 1868 a destructive
visitation of grasshoppers took place in the Red River
Settlement.   Any one who has not seen this locust invasion
cannot imagine it.   The pictures given by the Prophet
Joel were reproduced.   Myriads of voracious insects ate
up every green thing, and heaps of their dead, decaying
and putrid, filled the air with disgusting odors.

Sympathy in Britain and America was awakened for the
people left without food in Red River Settlement.   The
Hudson's Bay Company gave £6,000 stg. to relieve the
distress, and Canada sent her quota.   Mr. John Black, as a
member of the Relief Executive, took an active part in relieving the distress, and was in his element in comforting
the discouraged and the suffering.   The Canadian government determined on a plan of assistance which led to
serious complications, though at the time, it seemed

JUDICIOUS CHARITY.

The Canadian government thought it better to give public work to the destitute than to bestow indiscriminate charity.
Accordingly they undertook to build the wagon road
from Fort Garry to the Lake of the Woods, which has since
been known as the Dawson Road.   This was really a work
of much importance, the distance of 110 miles through the
wet country being much shorter than the long circuit by
Winnipeg River and Lake Winnipeg.   Though begun with
the most benevolent intention it was not long before the
question was raised by what right the Canadian government undertook it when they did not own the territory.

The Canadian agents, Messrs. Snow and Mair, who were
in charge of the work, paid all those who chose to work
upon the road, but there were questions as to the rate of
wages, method of payment, and the like, that became bitter
enough.

Trifling remarks of the contractors and their assistants,
as to the new state of affairs likely to come to the country,
to their seizure of land, and dispossession of the old settlers
and halfbreeds, were told about, and a very disagreeable
state of feeling was thus engendered.   " The Canadian
Party " was certainly most unwise in its attitude to the old
settlers of the country, though it is quite evident also that
unreasonable suspicion took possession of the people of
Red River.

The leaders of opinion in the settlement were, however,
in favor of the change to join fortunes with Canada.   Mr.
Black was most outspoken in favor of the advantage it
would be to have Canadian law established, and to be
brought in closer touch with his own church, and the

brethren from whom for twenty years he had been in a measure severed.

THE FLAME BURSTS OUT.

The negotiations between Canada and the Hudson's Bay Company had been favorable, the wide fields of the Northwest were to become Canadian, and a million and a half of dollars were to make up the loss to the veteran company. Hon. William McDougall was chosen as first Governor and was sent by way of Minnesota and Dakota to his new vice-royalty.

Suddenly one of the Canadian party, on October 22, 1869, appeared before the Master of Fort Garry and made affidavit that forty French halfbreeds, fully armed and equipped, had taken possession of the Queen's highway, some nine miles south of Fort Garry, and proposed to prevent Mr. McDougall, the new Governor, entering the colony. This startling news proved to be true and was a great surprise to the Company and to all the English-speaking people of Red River. All seemed paralyzed. Some were afraid of bloodshed, some thought the demonstration of the French was mere bravado, some that after a parley with the incoming Governor it would be arranged by his giving a promise of just treatment and equal rights. The inactivity of the civil authorities encouraged Riel, the French halfbreed leader of the unruly Metis.

Riel was a vain-glorious fellow, and he must do something brilliant. The party defending the "barriere" at St. Norbert began to tamper with the mails. Next, though most of his followers opposed it, Riel, by a *coup-de-main*, quartered a number of his men in the Fort, much to the disgust of the Hudson's Bay officers. Here again there was criminal inactivity on the part of the authorities.

Riel, the dictator, became still more bold, and issued a call to the parishes to send delegates to a meeting in the Fort. A show of opposition, even at this stage, on the part of the English-speaking people would probably have checked the insolent desperado at the Fort. The feeling of disgust on the part of the English at the impudent assumption of power by Riel was strong. Why, then, it may be asked, did not the spirit of their race assert itself at all hazards?

DIVIDED COUNSELS.

The answer is easily given. Jealousy and rivalry prevailed among the English speaking people themselves. The leader in the Canadian party was regarded as a selfish and unscrupulous man. He had for years instilled discontent through the columns of the *Nor'-Wester*. Many of the people of the settlement disliked him intensely. The incoming governor seemed to the people to be simply the shadow of this man. Colonel Dennis, the head of the surveying party was personally popular, but lacked penetration and decision. Had Governor McTavish, who unfortunately was in poor health, been able to make a call on the loyalty of the people, all would have been well, but this sentiment of distrust and dislike prevented it, and nothing was done. The Bishop of Rupert's Land declared he had gone to the first meeting of the Council of Assiniboine "prepared to recommend a forcible putting down of the insurrection." Mr. Black was as firm as any man could be against the arrogant impostor who held the Fort. Mr. Bannatyne, who understood the French people thoroughly, was forward in endeavoring to avert the disaster, but inaction, arising from mutual hatred, lost the opportunity, and encouraged by this, the French halfbreeds in the Fort grew to be six hundred in number.

TOO LATE.

Then it was too late. The Canadian garrison in Dr. Schultz's store but aggravated the feeling; the gathering of the English halfbreeds and others in Kildonan church only roused bitterness without accomplishing anything. It was useless to throw water on the fire, after standing and gazing listlessly at the blaze till it had grown strong. The stealing by Riel and his followers at the " barriere " of goods which were being imported to the settlement, the breaking open of the stores and looting the cellars of the Fort by his hungry horde, the killing of Scott, the suffering of the prisoners confined in Fort Garry, and the loud vapouring and personal insults of the insolent chief of the " New Nation " were part of the penalty inflicted on the people of the country, for the masterly inactivity arising from divided counsels, which had been shown. Mr. Black and the Highland parish stood sullenly by amazed and disgusted at the current of events. With few exceptions the whole parish would have responded to the call of authority, but the call never came. Mr. McDougall issued a proclamation when he was no Governor, Col. Dennis was divided in his mind and had no real authority, the true source of power— the Company—felt itself unable to act, and in the mean-time the rebellion triumphed.

THE COLLAPSE.

The rebellion had been agoing for two months, and Riel seemed at the summit of his power, when, two days after Christmas, Donald A. Smith, a prominent member of the

Hudson's Bay Company, arrived from Canada, at Fort
Garry. The Canadian government had realized its blunder,
and now sought to do by negotiation what it should have
done three months before. If instead of the hasty visit of
Hon. Joseph Howe, which itself did some good, two members of the government, one French and the other English,
had come up and conferred with the people, there would
have been no rebellion. It is so easy to be wise after the
event ! Mr. Smith was virtually a prisoner in Riel's hands,
was watched by him with suspicion, and was treated as dis-
courteously by the petty tyrant as he dared to do. How.
ever, by degrees, the Commissioner, who displayed great
tact as well as decision, began to sap the foundation of
Riel's authority. A monster meeting of the people was
held January 19th, in the open air at Fort Garry, with the
thermometer at 20 degrees below zero. Riel, with the true
instincts of a desperado, had seized a number of the papers
sent by the Governor-General of Canada. The mass meeting, however, resulted in a demand for the election of representatives to consider the invitation from Mr. Smith to
formulate their grievances.

One of the most useful and trusted men at this time in
the Red River settlement was A. G. B. Bannatyne, merchant and postmaster, in the village of Winnipeg, near Fort
Garry. Mr. Bannatyne was the real representative chosen
to the convention for Winnipeg, but an American mob by
force elected one of themselves. Mr. Bannatyne acted as
intermediary between the English and French, and long
after wielded much influence in Winnipeg. He was,
however, openly opposed to the leader of the Canadian
party.

Step by step the power of Riel waned until on the 4th of

March, probably to awe the people and regain his weakening power, he committed the desperate act of executing
Thomas Scott, a Canadian, contrary to the pleadings of
Donald A. Smith, Mr. Bannatyne and others. That was
the beginning of the end. The party to meet the Canadian
government, bearing a Bill of Rights, left soon after for
Ottawa. The news of the execution of Scott threw Canada
into a blaze. Ten thousand volunteers would have reported
in a day to go to Red River, if they had been called. The
name of Riel was despised and hated throughout the
English-speaking parishes and by many of the French.
The Canadian government busied itself in passing the
Manitoba Act, which established a province in a part of
Rupert's Land. The Wolseley expedition started as soon
as the spring opened, and the followers of Riel began
to leave him. The back of the rebellion was broken.
Late in August, 1870, the vanguard of the expedition
reached Fort Garry. Shortly before their arrival Riel and
two of his lieutenants left the Fort. The 6oth regiment
were anxious to have a brush with the rebels, but the three
captains, as the troops appeared in the distance, "folded
their tents like the Arabs and silently stole away."

RESTORING PEACE.

The coming of Governor Archibald and the establishment of Canadian institutions took place in the same year
as the arrival of the expedition. But it took years to establish peace. The writer came to Manitoba in the year after
this, and well remembers the bitterness and hatred which
continually showed themselves. The two old English-speaking factions struggled for supremacy. The influx of new
people in due time, however, overcame the feuds.

The sentiment against Riel and his associates burned as strongly years after as it did in the time of the troubles. Peace never came : eally until in Chief Justice Wood's court Riel and Lepine were found guilty of murder and sedition. The springs of action in communities are hard to trace, but it is plain to see that the burning questions which have agitated Manitoba, and through her the whole Dominion, since that time, have gained their intensity from the terrible months—for they were nothing short of that — from November to March, of the Red River rebellion.

Undoubtedly the heat of feeling of the "Canadian party" included for a time Mr. Black as being one of the other wing of the English-speaking people. But in his case this soon passed away. His personal character, his kindly and friendly manner, his open hospitality, and his unwavering loyalty to British institutions made new-comers find in the "Apostle of Red River" a friend, willing to aid all. Some of the more extreme of the so-called "Canadian party" attempted to misinterpret a casual remark of the good old pioneer to his disadvantage, but it was not accepted generally, and a few years after Mr. Black was as acceptable as a preacher to the rising congregation of Winnipeg as in his own beloved Kildonan. Often, often did he commiserate the people compelled to go through such an experience as that of 1869-70.

CHAPTER X.

The New Settlements.

To some, the story of early settlement appears pro-saic. To the deep thinking, there is in it romance of the most thrilling kind. Who has not read with sympathetic interest the story of Abraham going into a far country that God would tell him of? How Scottish hearts have been moved with the accounts of the Highland Clearances, when thousands of crofts and straths and glens were left behind, and their occupants hurried forth to find homes in Pictou, Glengarry, or on the banks of the Hudson !

It is not only in the painful separations, the leaving be-hind of spots and scenes consecrated with the dearest memories, and in some degree the sense of failure in hav-ing to give up old associations forced by hard necessity ; but the tearful outlook into the unknown, the dread of meeting the inhospitality of a cold world, and the utter feeling of uncertainty that give its human interest to the emigrant ship as it sails forth from the old-world port, or the settler's wagon as it wends its way through the bush or over the "interminable prairie."

All the pathetic scenes of early settlers' life became familiar in connection with the Red River becoming a part of
Canada. As soon as the Rebellion had been quelled, and
Manitoba became open for settlement, a movement took
place from all parts of Canada to occupy the fertile prairies
of the West. Farmers, whose families were finding the
small farm of one hundred acres or less on which they
had grown up too strait for them, sold off their possessions
and journeyed to Manitoba to take homesteads and pre-
emptions on its virgin prairies.

For the first few years the journey was made by rail to
St. Paul, in the American State of Minnesota. Here the
old-fashioned settler's wagon with its canvas top—the
prairie schooner as it has been called—was revived ; the
household goods and a stock of provisions were packed in
closely, and after them the women and children entered to
undertake a journey of nearly five hundred miles to the
new land of hope in the north. The father and sons drove
the herd of cattle and the extra horses ; and from camping
place to camping place groups of settlers' wagons moved in
daily caravans over the prairie trails.

In one such wagon the writer remembers to have seen
an old lady of over eighty years, who, seated in her com-
modious arm chair, held her post among the boxes and
bedding and farming tools over this long and weary route.
At a stopping place in the then utterly wild territory of
Dakota, the writer remembers to have seen the quaint
entry in the register of the wayside hostelry of J. W.,
"Citizen of the World." The traveller had evidently been
impressed with the illimitable stretch of the prairie, so like
the sea. At times the unbridged coulée, with its depth of
water, was to be crossed, when all the goods had to be un-

loaded from the wagons, the goods and chattels floated across, the horses and cattle made to swim over; and a delay, sometimes dangerous, of several hours checked the forward advance of the caravan. Sometimes the fierce storm of the prairie rose, and compelled the parties to keep camp for two or three days. The writer calls to mind one storm in 1872 that blew over tents, drove horses and cattle hither and thither over the prairies, and well-nigh brought bands of travellers to despair. Such are the dramatic features of frontier life.

At times the settler and his family went by rail as far as the Red River, and reached a town two hundred and twenty-five miles by land above Fort Garry. Here a Red River steamer was taken, and by following seven hundred miles of the winding river the destination was reached. The Red River steamer was of the Mississippi type, flat-bottomed and easily running over shallows. Indeed, speaking in western phrase, it could run over the prairie if there was a good heavy dew upon the grass. The extra goods were towed in barges behind the steamer, and old-timers still delight to recount the picturesque scenes connected with the Red River steamboat. At times, when the river had flooded its banks, the steamer lost her course in the night, and was compelled to fasten her bow to a tree on a prairie bluff till the morning. Thousands of the early settlers of Manitoba remember the river steamers—the delay of days together when stranded on the rapids—the wretched meals, and the primitive accommodation. Arrived at Fort Garry, the settler found the troubles and discomforts soon forgotten in the hurry and bustle of a new life.

Then the toilsome journey, on steamboat or over muddy roads, with myriads of mosquitoes and inevitable hardships, was past, and the steamer "tied up" at the warehouse, or the prairie caravan crossed the ferry of the Assiniboine and camped by the walls of Fort Garry. The sun seemed to shine all the brighter and the air was all the more exhilarating since the goal had been reached and the land of promise entered on.

At a distance of about half a mile from the fort was now springing up the straggling village of Winnipeg. This nucleus of the present city was a separate place, with different ideals and often divergent aspirations, from old Fort Garry. For years the struggle prevailed as to which should rule, but the increase of population, the influx of men of wider view, and the softening influence of time abolished the rivalries, and the Hudson's Bay Company has in late years entered into all the objects and prospects of the city along with its most enterprising citizens. The picture of that early Winnipeg is a strange contrast to the city of to-day.

Soon after his arrival the family patriarch and his stalwart sons found their way to the land office, inspected the list of vacant lands, ascertained where acquaintances had gone, and after visits and journeys hither and thither, made up their minds where to take up lands from the embarrassing plenty that was offered them. New townships were opening up in all directions where the surveyors had gone, and east and west new settlements sprang up like magic.

The Kildonan people, from their greater intelligence than that of their neighbors, and their long residence in the country, were naturally much consulted as to the best parts of the country and the localities most desirable for settlement. Their habits of life, however, being more pastoral than agricultural, had led them to different views from those taken by the majority of the new-comers who were farmers. The writer remembers very well in 1871 hearing of several Canadian families, who had broken the immemorial custom of settling along the river bank, and had ventured beyond Bird's Hill on the one hand, and Stony Mountain on the other, several miles from the river. These were looked upon by some of the old settlers as simply mad, their failure was prophesied, and the expectation was strongly held that they would be frozen on the plains, or lost in the snow-drifts if they attempted during the winter to find their way to the old settlement. To-day, tens of thousands of Manitoba settlers have their comfortable houses on the open plains.

SOUND THE GOSPEL CLARION.

Wherever the settler goes, there must the herald of the Gospel follow him. Many of the early settlers of Manitoba came from the congested agricultural districts of Bruce, Huron and Lanark counties, in Ontario. As these were strongly Presbyterian localities, a very large proportion of the incoming settlers belonged to the church whose foundation John Black had been for twenty years so industriously and firmly laying. The Presbytery of Manitoba had been formed just in time (1870) to deal with this great influx of people, and applications came to it from almost every new locality to have the Gospel preached. It was a great responsibility. Money and men were scarce, and the source of both these lay in the older provinces, from which so many of the older settlers were coming. The doctrine was laid down that it was the duty of settled pastors, ordained missionaries, college professors, students and also efficient elders, to occupy the new and rising settlements, and the leading members of Presbytery cherished it as an ambition to be the first church to preach the Gospel in each rising settlement. That ambition has been largely fulfilled in the quarter of a century that has elapsed since it was formed. It involved great self-denial to accomplish this. But the spirit prevailed. It has led to the enormous growth that has taken place, as seen in the fact that the nine preaching places of 1870 have increased to the vast number, north and west of Lake Superior, of 839 in 1897.

CHURCH STATESMANSHIP.

Much more, however, than this was necessary. The new province of Manitoba was unknown. People do not send their contributions largely to places of which they know nothing. There were many in the eastern provinces who had no confidence in the future of Manitoba. One of the leaders of the Church denounced it as a frozen Siberia, and declared himself unwilling to spend a dollar of mission money within its hyperborean limits.

It became the duty of John Black and his colleagues to do away with this false notion. They knew well their advantage as belonging to the Presbyterian Church. It is a church which legislates in its highest court—the General Assembly—for the weak as well as for the strong ; for the maligned as well as for the popular ; for the distant as well as for the central interests. Accordingly the Manitoba men began the work by letter, and full report, and map, and speech, and personal influence, with the purpose of letting the church know the capabilities of the country, and the prospect of a large population coming to cultivate its fertile soil.

And this was not a mere spasmodic effort, but it has

continued from that day to this. The Presbytery of Manitoba kept up a constant agitation as to its wants, knowing that the kindly mother in the east but needed to hear the cry of her children and she would relieve them. And so it has been. The outlook of the church has been so widened that to day money flows freely to Manitoba, Assiniboia, Alberta, Saskatchewan and British Columbia for the wide mission work of the west.

HARD WORK.

But the organization and development of the work in the new settlements was a mighty task. In Mr. Black's letters are frequently found : " Received your letter as I was leaving to visit Grassmere "; " Have just returned from the new settlement in Springfield "; " Paid a visit on church work to the Portage," and the like. This was to an equal or larger extent the same with every ordained missionary, professor and other laborer. The great question became, Who could do the most, not, Who could escape the most. The work was carried on during the winter as thoroughly as in summer.

In 1874 one of the ministers undertook to supply a new settlement, forty miles from Winnipeg, once a month during winter. Preaching at the distant point on Sabbath morning he came towards the city, about half way took another service among people who had come in that very year, and then struck homeward across the treeless, pathless, uninhabited prairie, having nothing to guide him but the stars.

The roads over the prairie in early days were nothing but trails running in a most perplexing manner, and missionaries were constantly losing their way, and sometimes spent the night in the shelter of a bluff, or solitary stack in the wide hay meadow. In some years the roads were very bad. To become " mired " or " bogged " in a " slough," and to have the shaganappi or Indian pony coolly lie down in the mud, was an occurrence by no means uncommon. Winter with its biting blasts gave no respite to the faithful missionary.

The history of Manitoba missions has been a marvellous record of faithful, uncomplaining, self-denying service. Men have been placed in charge of six or seven townships with settlers scattered sparsely through them. They have carried on for years, in winter's cold and summer's heat, service at six and seven points, three and even four on a Sabbath, and all this on small and poorly paid stipends. Truly Christ said, " My kingdom is not of this world."

THE HONOR ROLL.

Did time and general interest permit, the growth from year to year, and from district to district, in Manitoba might be traced ; the special work of faithful missionaries might be given and their great services recounted. This is not our present purpose. The presbytery, in its early missionary plans in 1871, consisted of Revs. John Black, James Nisbet, William Fletcher, John McNabb, and the writer. Mr. Nisbet was five hundred miles west, at Prince Albert, and the little knot of members seemed too small to face so large a work ; but missionary after missionary was sent by the generous and patriotic home mission committee in Toronto. Prof. Hart, a missionary of the Church of Scotland in Canada, came to join us in the following year, and Rev. James Robertson two years after that.

WINNIPEG IN 1870.

Frazer, Matheson, Donaldson, and Vincent were active members of presbytery and worthy foundation builders. McKellar, Bell and Stewart were a trio who did yeoman service in the splendid farming region of Portage la Prairie and Gladstone. Scott and Borthwick and Ross took hold of Southern Manitoba and laid the foundations of numerous congregations, such as Emerson, Carman, Morden and others, now self-sustaining and influential. Alex. Campbell, James Douglas, A. H. Cameron, and Alexander Smith all earned a good degree in the later seventies, and are still residents of the west. Such men as McGuire, Wellwood, Donald McRae, Hodnett, and Polson were hard-working pioneers in the last years in which John Black yet remained with us.

St. Paul's list of worthies was well called a cloud of witnesses in his wonderful chapter in the Hebrews, and we honor those whose names have become world-wide for their faith and self-sacrifice ; but many of the names now mentioned are also those of men of unflinching courage, of splendid endurance, of godly lives, and truest influence. The fact that numbers of them, and others who have since come to the west, were willing to bury themselves in obscure mission stations for the sake of Christ, but showed them to be men of the same spirit as John Black, and their virtues call for admiration and regard.

SPECIAL DIFFICULTIES.

The great mission work, from 1871 to 1881, was of the most difficult and trying kind. The settlements were new, the people were very scattered, were strangers to one another, their resources were small, and mission work was carried on under the greatest disadvantages. But such faithful, self-denying work never goes unrewarded. During one-half of this decade the country suffered from the terrible plague of the grasshoppers. The new farmers all through the settlements were greatly discouraged. About the year 1875 there were thousands of settlers of Manitoba reduced to the scantiest fare. The writer recalls those dark days of the new settlement.

If ever the consolations of religion were needed, and indeed largely appreciated, it was during the years of the grasshopper scourge. The services were held in settlers' houses. The settlers kindly invited the missionaries after service to share their scanty fare, and many a time the missionary felt ashamed to be a burden on those who were literally suffering from the lack of sufficient food. The settlers were, however, in a country from which they had not means to return to their eastern homes, and so, ragged and hungry, they were compelled to wait to be delivered by a Higher Hand. In 1876 the last grasshoppers left Manitoba, and gradually the new settlements have risen, till now neatly built Presbyterian churches dot the landscape in all quarters of Manitoba, and the sacrifice of pioneer missionaries, elders and people has been rewarded.

EARLY WINNIPEG.

Perhaps the most picturesque and successful example of mission effort was that in what was at the beginning of the period the village of Winnipeg. For years before the transfer of the Red River country to Canada service had been held by Mr. Black in the Court House near Fort Garry. There had been little growth. The expectation roused by the new state of things led to the erection of a small Presbyterian church in the village. John Black obtained some

$400 assistance from Canada, and erected a wooden build ing, 30 x 40 feet. This building, yet unfinished, but suffi ciently advanced to be used, was opened for public worship by Rev. Dr. Black on December 3rd, 1868.

The completion of this building was interfered with by the Rebellion of 1869-70, but the arrival of the troops and the coming of a few Canadians led to the partial fitting up of the church in 1870, a committee consisting mostly of the officers and men of the volunteer force doing the work necessary. A view of the cut given herewith will show the appearance of the church. The original intention was to have a tower on the top, and in the sketch the timbers are shown which were to have been the mainstays. For a year these posts were an eyesore to the community, but one night they disappeared. It is said that the sexton, acting on a hint from some quarter, clambered on the roof and removed the offending posts.

The interior of the church was somewhat ambitious for those times. The pulpit had a high Gothic backpiece, in harmony with the churchly windows to be seen in the sketch. The committee of the troops in 1870 partitioned off a portion of the interior as ante-rooms, and left the church seated for about one hundred and fifty persons. To this little building John Black gave the name Knox church, in memory of the mother church in Toronto, of which Dr. Burns, the patron of the Red River mission, had been pastor.

KNOX CHURCH ORGANIZED.

In October, 1871, the writer was placed in charge of Knox church, and regular services twice a day were begun. John Black took the most lively interest in everything connected with the congregation. He knew that it repre-

KNOX CHURCH, WINNIPEG, 1871.

sented the movement in a city which was to become the central fortress of Presbyterianism in Manitoba and in all the far west. The congregation was organized in 1872 with eleven members, and a session was elected in the following year. In 1874 the congregation had grown to have seventy-three members, and unanimously called Rev. James Robertson, of Norwich, Ontario, and though small in numbers guaranteed a salary of $2,000 per annum. In 1872 the church building had been enlarged, again in 1873 and a third addition took place in 1875. During the pastorate of Mr. Robertson, which lasted seven years, there was a large immigration to the province. Knox church grew very rapidly. Mr. Robertson was a most faithful pastor, and took an especial interest in the incoming population. He was ever willing to give a helping hand to the lonely or discouraged newcomer. Knox church has ever been known as a great supporter of the home mission work of the Church.

As has been well said: "The greatest enterprise in which the congregation engaged, in addition to its regular and missionary work in Mr. Robertson's pastorate, was the new Knox church building. This is known as the second Knox church. This was largely accomplished through the energy and personal effort of the pastor. Indeed so sedulously did the pastor work up the subscription list, that it has been said that it was in this that Mr. Robertson laid the foundation of the great success that he has since gained in finances as Superintendent of Missions." The congregation had in 1879 grown to have four hundred names upon the roll, and thus desired to have a more comfortable place of worship. The second Knox church, as will be seen from the accompanying illustration, was a handsome and commanding building. In August, 1881, the first colony from Knox church went off to form St. Andrew's church. This was placed in the northern part of the city, and was begun just in time to meet the great railway population which came in in connection with the Canadian Pacific Railway. It was ministered to by the Rev. C. B. Pitblado. These two congregations represented the Presbyterianism of Winnipeg during the life of Dr. Black, but he always believed in the growth of Winnipeg. How greatly he would have rejoiced could he have lived to see the handful he had nursed and seen begun as a congregation in the little wooden church with eleven members, develop into seven self-sustaining congregations and two missions, with nine church buildings in all to-day, numbering two thousand five hundred and fifty-four communicants in the city of Winnipeg.

As we have said before, it has often been spoken of regretfully by the friends of the pioneer that John Black was taken away just when the fuller measure of the success of Presbyterianism in the great west was dawning. However, Simeon-like, he was satisfied. He lived to see the foundations well laid in the new settlements, including the new city of the prairies. He saw the mission work become too large for management by the ordinary machinery of the presbytery. He was quite in sympathy with his brethren as to the necessity of a special agent being set apart to superintend the rapidly rising missions, and when Dr. Robertson was unanimously chosen as superintendent of missions, though Mr. Black regretted his being taken from Knox church congregation, yet he rejoiced in the appointment and gave his heartiest congratulation to the new superintendent. Dr. Robertson had just begun his work, which has yielded such a magnificent fruitage to the cause of Christ in the West, while the good pastor of Kildonan was struggling for health in the last few months of his life. How often do we see the true, the good, the noble, thus

> " By affliction touched and saddened."

> " But the glories so transcendant
>   That around their memories cluster,
>   And on all their steps attendant,
>   Make their darkened lives resplendent
>   With such gleams of inward lustre."

KNOX CHURCH, WINNIPEG, 1879.

MANITOBA COLLEGE, 1872.

CHAPTER XI.

College and Schools.

Next to John Black's desire for the spiritual good of the people among whom he labored, was his anxiety for the education of the young. Born in Scotland, where to be illiterate is looked upon as disgraceful; brought up under teachers in the parish school, who had a real love of knowledge and whose joy it was to select from their pupils every "lad of pairts"; afterwards well trained in a higher institution in New York State; and having finished his course in Canada at a time when a new educational impulse led to the founding of Knox College, the pastor of Kildonan could scarcely fail to be

AN EDUCATIONIST.

His bent of mind constantly showed itself in his desire to help forward promising youths. It was not enough to him that the parish school of Kildonan should be the best in the Red River Settlement. He took those who were looking forward to professional life, and in his own study drilled them in the Latin and Greek classics, with which he was so familiar. A number of the Kildonan lads went on to higher positions, led in their earlier stages by his kindly hand.

Higher educational facilities were not wanting to Kildonan, for upon the borders of the parish, and beside the very church where until 1851 the fathers of the Kildonan people had attended public worship, was St. John's College. Here a good education was given, and, so far as known to the writer, there were no restrictions placed upon those students who were not members of the Church of England ; but John Black desired to mould the leaders of the Presbyterian people after a fashion to preserve the best traditions of the race from which they sprang.

The small number of people in the Red River Settlement, and their remoteness from highly civilized life, was for a time an objection to the founding of another college on the banks of the Red River. Now, however, the vista of hope was opening out before the couutry, as a new province was entering on its career as one of the Canadian sisterhood. The Kildonan school reached the culmination of its excellence during the years 1870 and 1871 under the direction of Mr. David B. Whimster, a teacher from western Ontario. The attendance was large, the educational interest was great, and a goodly number of the best pupils were being instructed in Latin and French by Mr. Black. Now seemed the time for carrying out the dream which the Kildonan pastor had long cherished.

THE COLLEGE PLANNED.

In the autumn of 1870, the very year in which the young province of Manitoba was born, a provisional board of twelve of the leading Presbyterians of the province signed a prospectus and circulated it through the province inviting assistance for an institution to give a training in Classics, Mathematics, Chemistry, Natural History, Moral and Mental Philosophy, and the Modern Languages. We may certainly say there was no restricted view in the minds of the founders of the infant college. Early ' in 1871, £300 sterling had been subscribed on the Red River, and before the meeting of the General Assembly material for the new building had been secured and the building was expected to be sufficiently advanced for use in the autumn of the year.

The General Assembly met that year in Quebec, and the Rev. William Fletcher, a commissioner from Manitoba, strongly presented the case for the new college.

THE ASSEMBLY DECIDES.

As usual " some doubted," but the Assembly entered with spirit upon the project, and after certain negotiations the writer was appointed to go to Manitoba and lay the foundations of the new institution. He was ordained for the work in Gould Street church, Toronto, in company with Dr. MacKay of Formosa, and pushed on to reach Manitoba before winter. After a long and toilsome journey, in October the writer arrived at Red River, and looks back with pleasure to the first night spent in company with John Black at Kildonan manse. The Rev. William Fletcher and the writer on arriving at Fort Garry could find no accommodation in the crowded hotel in Winnipeg, and accordingly they walked down the four miles or more to the manse on a pleasant autumn evening.

The Apostle of the Red River, with a mass of iron gray hair, as shown in his portrait, with well marked and yet kindly face, and his Dumfrieshire Doric, not yet displaced

9

by forty years of absence from his native moorlands, was
in high spirits. So often had the people of Red River
seen those coming to them foiled in their plans by the too
early approach of winter that their fears had been awakened
lest another disappointment would reach them. But the
journey had been made, and now the pioneer, whose tastes
had always remained scholastic and literary, even in the
remote solitudes of the west, saw one of his strongest anti-
cipations about to be realized. He spoke of the youths
ready to go on with their work, of the numbers coming into
the country, of the bright prospects of the Church, and the
value of education as a factor of national growth. Late
into the night all phases of the subject were discussed
and plans laid for immediately beginning work.

MANITOBA COLLEGE BEGUN.

A few days afterward the provisional board met, and the
name " Manitoba College " was adopted for the new institution—a name which has meant much in the educational
development of the western prairies. On November 10th,
1871, classes were opened, and the work immediately took
hold of the minds and hearts of the Presbyterian people of
the country, and of many others as well. The first building was of logs covered with siding, and so Manitoba College while not emulating the fame of the log college, out
of which great Princeton College grew, yet has a similarity in
its first housing and surroundings. The cut on page 130
gives a view of the first college building at Kildonan, with
the Kildonan church in the background.

In the year following the opening of the college the staff
was strengthened by the arrival of the Rev. Thomas Hart,
B. D., who was the representative of the Church of Scotland

in Canada. Professor Hart came under an arrangement with the Church of Scotland Synod to take part in the educational work, and has in the quarter of a century since his coming labored with unwearied diligence for the good of the college. The co-operation of the two branches of the Church in college work three years before the union of the Churches proved the advisability of the scheme of union, and was the harbinger of that event which has been such a blessing to religion throughout the Dominion of Canada.

REMOVAL TO WINNIPEG.

The college steadily progressed for two sessions, when an event took place which seriously tried the stability and attachment to principle of the Presbyterians of the country, more especially of the people of Kildonan. This was nothing less than the proposed removal of the newly-founded college from Kildonan to Winnipeg. There can be no doubt that this was one of the most trying things to Mr. Black in his whole experience. Kildonan was four or five miles distant from the rising capital of the province. Three miles nearer the city than Manitoba College stood St. John's College. The Methodist Church had opened an academy in the heart of Winnipeg, and the disadvantages of fair development under which Manitoba College lay at Kildonan were manifest. The matter came up in the Presbytery of Manitoba, and the scheme favorable to beginning work in the provincial centre was carried by the casting vote of the Moderator. It was naturally a great grief to the people of Kildonan, and especially to their earnest pastor. To see the longed-for tree of knowledge so speedily plucked up by the roots seemed to the good old pioneer unnatural and uncalled for. And yet it was the struggle

between reason and sentiment. The good of the institution itself and the plan to be adopted for its greatest usefulness must be the highest considerations. The matter was
necessarily taken to the General Assembly. Mr. Black had
not intended to be present that year at the General
Assembly, but at the wish of Kildonan itself went in order
that he might give the view of the people against the removal of the college. All who were present at that Assembly will remember the address of the valiant representative.
With singular clearness and the highest dignity, though with
deep emotion, he recounted the struggles of the people of
Kildonan, the sacrifices they had made for the Church and
country, the hopes that had been awakened, and the dam-
age it would do the college among the relatively small number of Presbyterians yet settled in the country. The
Assembly was deeply impressed by the appeal of the devoted and unselfish advocate. The writer recalls the fact of
one of the most respected pillars of the church, Hon. John
McMurrich, coming to him privately and saying, " I quite
agree with the argument in favor of removing the college
to the rising town, but it does seem hard that after all the
struggles of the faithful pioneers of Presbyterianism on the
Red River, and especially after the devoted and self-sacrificing life that John Black has lived, that there can be
found no way in which their wishes may be gratified."
There was not a member of the General Assembly who did
not feel in the same way as good old John McMurrich.
But it was a critical moment in the history of northwestern
Presbyterianism. To have hesitated at that time would
have been to take up the same movement in a few years
again with the added difficulty of a falling cause and a
sense of failure.

DEPUTATION SENT.

The Assembly acted with extreme caution and discern-
ment in the matter. A commission of two of its members,
Drs. Ure, of Goderich, and Cochrane, of Brantford, the
former an old fellow-student and warm friend of Mr. Black,
was appointed to visit Manitoba and report upon the case.
The commission decided that after a year the college should
be removed to Winnipeg, and carry on its whole work there.
This was naturally a great disappointment to Mr. Black.
He was not convinced by the decision, and feared especially that hurt would be done the college among the old
settlers of the country. He quoted in confirmation of his
opinion the statement made by the Bishop of Rupert's
Land, the head of St. John's College, that the removal was
a mistake.

In this John Black, to his own surprise and happiness also,
found himself mistaken. The Kildonan people, to their
infinite credit, stood true to their principles and in the next
and succeeding years, numbers of their young men were educated in their own college in Winnipeg, notwithstanding
their feeling of disappointment at the loss of the college.
Acting in the same manner as he had done when his views
were not carried out in regard to the policy of managing the
Prince Albert mission, the true-hearted Presbyterian pastor
still gave his unwavering support to the college, and for
several years when the college undertook the instruction of
a small band of theological students, came, in company with
Dr. Robertson, at considerable inconvenience to himself,
and unrewarded except by the gratitude of the board and
the high appreciation of the students, to deliver lectures in
church history of which he was so complete a master. It
was with the deepest appreciation of his scholarship and

high character that the Board of Manitoba College congrat-
ulated him in 1876, when the sister institution in the Church,
Queen's College, conferred the degree of Doctor of Divinity
upon the one who had been the originator and strong sup-
porter of general and theological education among the
Presbyterians of the western prairies.

THE UNIVERSITY ESTABLISHED.

The college continued to grow and, after the union of
1875, obtained a building of its own in the northern part of
Winnipeg. It became in 1877, along with the Church of
England College of St. John and the Roman Catholic College of St. Boniface, a part of the University of Manitoba,
which was established in that year.   From the first it took
the lead in the University of Manitoba, and to-day has upwards of one hundred and eighty graduates in Arts.   Dr.
Black was among the earliest representatives of the college
on the council of the university.   The needs of the college
became so great that in 1881 the beautiful college building
represented in the accompanying cut was erected at a cost
of $40,000.   The Marquis of Lorne laid the corner stone
of the new college.   Dr. Black lived to see the erection of
the building, but passed away too soon to witness its occu-
pation in the autumn of 1882.

The difficulties of the college were many during these
early years.   As has been said, "this part of its history was
the period of uncertainty, and of many sleepless nights for
its professors.   Eleven or twelve years of no visible means
of support, of inevitable friction, arising from the necessary
change from Kildonan to Winnipeg, of an utterly insuf-
ficient staff for undertaking the university work in which it
early took part, and of its professors each weighted down

with as much missionary work as an ordinary missionary, to enable them to gain remuneration from the Home Mission Committee—these were the struggles of development with which the young organism grew into strength." No one was more sympathetic than John Black in encouraging the professors in their toil.

During its whole history Manitoba College has been a missionary centre for the west. The authorities of the college have always been anxious to make the college in every way useful to the Church. Its professors have taken a very active part in the home mission work and Indian missions, and its students have been strongly possessed with the missionary spirit. Before the college had the status of a theological college, in co-operation with the Presbytery of Manitoba, it gave instruction to students in theology with the approval of the General Assembly. In the year following that of the death of Dr. Black, Manitoba College was granted a regular theological department, and this part of the college work has been well organized and maintained under Dr. King and Professor Baird. No less than 81 graduates in theology have left the walls of the college between 1878 and the present time (1897). In token of its absorbing interest in home mission work, Manitoba College has willingly placed itself at the service of the Church in conducting a summer session in theology, for the better supply of the mission stations of the synods of Manitoba and British Columbia. Dr. Black would have greatly rejoiced, could he have seen the present prosperity of the institution for which he prayed and labored so long.

PUBLIC SCHOOLS.

The change made by the first parliament of Manitoba from the denominational schools formerly prevailing to a system of public schools was a very striking one. The desire of the Roman Catholics to have separate schools for themselves was granted, and thus the germ of the great question which has for years disturbed Manitoba was introduced. Those, who in the old Red River Settlement days had been accustomed to their parish schools, were not seriously opposed to the separate school system. To them it seemed simply a more systematic way of working their parish schools, and receiving the assistance of a government grant. Dr. Black thus became the representative of the Presbyterian parishes and was a member of the first Board of Education for the province. Matters worked with a fair amount of smoothness, but there was a constant grasping of power by the Roman Catholic hierarchy to make a greater and greater division between the two sections of the board, until in ten years after the formation of the province the Roman Catholic schools were to all intents and purposes managed privately by the Catholic section of the board, and the Roman Catholic Archbishop recognized as the authority by whom, for his own section, all books in religion and morals should be approved. Protests in the newspapers, in political campaigns and otherwise were made against this gradual aggression on the part of the Roman Catholics.

ACTION TAKEN.

The Protestant section of the board at length took action in the matter. A series of resolutions were passed on Oct. 4th, 1876, by a majority of the section, looking toward the doing away of separate schools. The matter promised to bring on a great agitation in the country, and Dr. Black ceased to be a member of the board, though Rev. Dr.

Robertson, who was also a Presbyterian representative on the board, held with the majority and ardently approved of the national school ideas. Dr. Black in this matter felt that he could not be a party to interfere with the amity be. tween Protestants and Roman Catholics, which had been a feature of the old days of the Red River Settlement. While he probably differed little from the other members of the board as to what should be done, yet his strongly expressed desire to be freed from the personal turmoil and discussion of this difficult question was regarded, and the burden thrown on younger men.

THE GOVERNMENT INTERFERES.

The Provincial Government of the time became alarmed at the action of the Protestant section of the board, and took the strong measure of reconstituting the board at the time of next appointment. Some of the more aggressive members were replaced by others of a more pacific charac. ter and the crisis was thus posponed. Dr. Black's antici- pations of the reality of this struggle were by no means mistaken. For several years the question slumbered, with, in 1881, a new aggression on the part of the Roman Catholics, making the two systems more distinct and main- taining the share of joint stock company assessments, which were almost entirely those of Protestant stockholders, *pro rata* for Roman Catholic schools. Dr. Black's fears of trouble were soon to be realized, for after ominous rumb- lings, on the incoming of a new government, in a few years the educational change took place (1890), giving rise to what has been widely known throughout the world as the " Manitoba School Question." Dr. Black died a number of years before this reformation came about.

CHAPTER XII

Memorials.

In the thirtieth year of Mr. Black's ministry a con-siderable religious movement took place in Winnipeg and the neighboring country. Mr. Black's interest in vital religion was ever one of his outstanding features. His conception of the Christian minister was that he was in reality a shepherd of the flock. It was his high mission to study the times and the seasons and to avail himself of any wise and timely circumstances which might arise in connection with the religious life of the parish.

The influx of a large number of new settlers can hardly be said to have had a favorable influence on the Highland parish. The life of the colonist or settler, even when he is well disposed, is likely to lead to carelessness in religious things, to laxity in the observance of the Sabbath, and to exposure to many temptations. Kildonan parish, being near Winnipeg, and much in touch with the new settlers, was thus exposed to hurtful influences. As a wise watch-man, the pastor of Kildonan saw this, and gladly welcomed tokens of spiritual revival, and took part very heartily in the movement to have special services in his beloved parish. We are fortunate in having a sermon of the pastor on the subject of revivals, published some years before the time of which we are speaking.

Referring to

REVIVALS,

Mr. Black says : "Happy the ministers thus privileged to be instruments in God's hand. Happy the souls who plentifully partake of this extraordinary grace! And it is well worth remembering how beautifully this mode of dealing with men is adapted to the wants and weaknesses of the race.

"Not only do spiritual affections become languid and require to be freshened with new life, but even the very ideas and impressions of a spiritual and eternal world wax dim upon the soul through the lapse of time, and the influence of the world and something extraordinary is required to renew these—some fresh testimony that there is a God and an eternity.

"It must be familiar to all, how events and appearances, however stupendous in themselves, lose their impressions by such regular recurrence as renders them familiar to our minds. What, for instance, can present a more magnificent spectacle than the passage of the sun through the heavens on a clear summer day? Yet so familiar are we with the spectacle that we scarcely think of it. It is a part of the regular operations of nature and passes unobserved.

"But suppose some day that the sun should appear of double size, or that another sun of equal brilliancy were to traverse the heavens from north to south, then all would be struck and filled with amazement—it may be with alarm —for then it would appear that there is some power superior to nature that can interfere with its regular course when he will. God would thus be brought near.

"So it is in spiritual things; however mightily the work of God might be carried on, men would soon begin to forget God in it, and to attribute the deep and earnest religious feelings prevailing to natural causes, and so something higher still would be needed to prove that the work was of God. Much more is this needed in a time of comparative indifference to bring palpably before men's minds that there is a God and a spiritual world. Men require something uncommon to stir them up from to time. Our private devotions would be more ready to sink into coldness and apathy were they not quickened by the public services of the sanctuary, and the Sabbath services would also degenerate, were we not stirred up by the occasional occurrence of Sacramental services. So God's ordinary dealings require the aid of these seasons of revival."

SOME DROPS DESCEND.

The meetings, as conducted by the evangelist in Kildonan church, were attended with good. There was much in the manner of the professional evangelist that did not commend itself to the more staid religious customs of Kildonan, but Dr. Black and his session, being in earnest in the cure of souls, overlooked the defects and sought to make the most of the efforts of the messenger of God sent amongst them. A considerable quickening took place among the young people, and the older people were helped as well. This was a great joy to the pastor. The strain upon the faithful minister in his person was, however, very great. The frequency of the services and the feeling of responsibility told upon his deeply moved nature, and by the time the meetings were ended the godly man was prostrated in body. Rest was tried, and a visit to thè Province of Ontario was undertaken, but without very much permanent benefit.

The good old apostle took advantage of his eastern visit to attend the meeting of the General Assembly in Kingston in 1881. He was expected to be present at it, and it seemed to be the desire of the leading ministers of the Church that the honor of the Moderatorship should be conferred on Dr. Black, as no less than ten presbyteries had nominated him. On the opening of Assembly a letter was read from Dr. Black, declining, on account of his poor health, to be put in nomination for this exalted position.

A HIGH ESTIMATE.

The grounds for the proposed honor were not only the fact that John Black was the first missionary to the Red River, but that he had so well fulfilled the functions of pastor, preacher, and leader. Few had, indeed, heard the apostle of Red River, but it was well-known that he was a preacher of no mean order. His reputation as a theologian was well established, an evangelical tone was highly characteristic of his sermons, and his fervid appeals and denunciation of wrong-doing were telling, while a poetic and eloquent power of expression was certainly possessed by him in his nobler efforts. As an example of his successful preaching, we may refer to a very effective and touching sermon delivered by him in the earlier part of his ministry.

Among the youths who had gone from Red River to study, we have already mentioned Donald Fraser. He was a young man of singularly attractive disposition, who as a boy had suffered from a disease in the hip joint. Recover-

ing somewhat, he had gone on with his education, and had
in 1854 entered Knox College, Toronto, where he continued a student for three years. It is said of him that in
addition to his more than ordinary ability and diligence, he
was distinguished for "his deep and steady, yet gentle,
cheerful, unobtrusive piety." On his return to Red River,
the disease increased, and attended by the kindly and continuous spiritual care of his minister, in the late winter he
passed away, joyfully exclaiming, "I am going to glory."
Ardently attached to his young friend, the Kildonan pastor
preached a beautiful sermon on Rev. vii. 1, 3, 14, entitled,

"FROM TRIBULATION TO GLORY."

We may well give an extract or two :
"How many have been thus removed who seemed the
very men to labor for God here ! This is the Lord's doing.
It is marvellous in our eyes." It is mysterious, yet we can
see reason in it—the Lord will show that He is not dependent on men. And there is mercy in it—He spares the
green and takes the ripe. To our departed brother the
change is unspeakable gain—he is gone forth out of all his
tribulations. Faith is changed into sight, hope into enjoyment. He is gone to see the Saviour, whom long he had
trusted and long loved. Faith, we may be well sure (a favor-
ite form of speech of John Black), had many a struggle to
realize a present Redeemer ; but now there is no struggle ;
he sees Him as He is, and is like Him. We are left. His
form is no longer before our eyes. But in his meekness
and gentleness of disposition, in his Christian consistency
and cheerfulness, in his patience under suffering, in his
prayerfulness and faithfulness, and in his kindness of heart
and spirituality of mind, he has left us an example which

woe unto us if we forget. And in his happy, joyful death-bed, unvisited by doubt or fear, we have another blessed evidence of the reality of religion and the faithfulness of God. To the family the loss is great, but their sorrow is mingled with joy, for not the shadow of doubt is left upon their minds. To myself the loss is also great. There I found sympathy, counsel, encouragement, prayer. But that heart and those lips are now still.

"IN ROBES OF WHITE."

"See these glorious, these shining ones, walking in brightness the golden streets of the New Jerusalem. They are clothed in white robes—angels' garments. Such was the clothing of our Lord on the day of His transfiguration, and such was the clothing of the angel that rolled the stone away from the door of His tomb."

THE WHITE ROBE IS THE EMBLEM OF PURITY.

The white robe without signifies the pure and holy heart within. These are purified, holy souls. In them has been fulfilled to the utmost, David's prayer : " Purge me with hyssop and I shall be clean ; wash me and I shall be whiter than snow." No stain of guilt now remains upon their consciences, no stain of corruption now defiles their hearts ; no sinful desire, no vile or tumultuous passion now agitates their minds. Their thoughts are all pure ; their affections are all heavenly ; they are conformed to the image and the will of God. Not the smallest thing in them is out of keeping with the holy heaven in which they now dwell.

THE WHITE ROBE IS ALSO AN EMBLEM OF JOY.

It is the wedding garment—the dress of the bride, the

Lamb's wife—the garment of the guests that sit at the heavenly banquet. The white robe without signifies the joyful heart within. And, oh, a happy company are all these white-robed ones in their Heavenly Father's home! The sorrows of earth are all left behind, and not even the shadow of evil now obscures the sunshine of their holy joys. No sin, no sorrow, no care, no toil, no fear, no conflict; but purity, peace, delight—their Father's smile, their Saviour's presence, the society of the redeemed and of holy angels, the sight of heavenly beauty, the sounds of heavenly music, the fragrance of celestial flowers, the sweetness of the water of life, the exercises of heavenly devotion, all conspiring to fill their minds with gladness ineffable. The marriage robe without is the emblem of the joyful heart within.

THE WHITE ROBE IS THE EMBLEM OF VICTORY.

It was worn by those who after victory returned to the Imperial city and passed in triumphal procession through the crowded streets, and the admiring and shouting multitudes. Those who have entered the New Jerusalem have gained the victory; they now enjoy the triumph. They have fought the good fight; they have finished their course, they have kept the faith; henceforth they are to enjoy their crowns of righteousness, their white robes, and their evergreen palms. Long and hard was the conflict; many and fierce were their enemies; but now the victory is won—sin, Satan and the world are subdued; and the sword and the breastplate, the buckler and the shield have been exchanged for the white robes of victory and of peace. "They hang their trumpet in the hall and study war no more."

OUT OF AFFLICTION.

" Many are the afflictions of the righteous, but the Lord delivereth him out of them all." They were in pain, in sickness, in poverty, in hunger, thirst, and nakedness ; they were exposed to shame, they were oppressed by tyranny ; they have been captives, slaves, victims of cruelty and in-justice ; they have seen their dearest snatched from their embraces ; they have passed through the trials which are common to man, and many peculiar to themselves ; but they have come out of all their tribulations—sickness and pain, captivity and bereavement, oppression and suffering are now forever ended, and God has wiped away all tears from their eyes."

A BELOVED ELDER.

We have before us another address of Mr. Black worthy of being quoted. This was delivered on the death of one of his best beloved elders, John Pritchard. This elder was the son of an English fur trader of the same name, who had been in the service of the Northwest Fur Company, and afterward acted as Lord Selkirk's agent. The tender heart of John Black comes out in his words for his depart-ed friend : " John Pritchard was a man of God. In him we have lost a man of much prayer—of deep humility, and one who knew well how to speak the truth in love, and who in his deportment beautifully mingled the gravity and the cheerfulness of true religion—a gravity without gloom or austerity—a cheerfulness without levity—a mingling or union of qualities which gave him at once the respect of the aged and the confidence of the young.

" In him his family have lost a wise, faithful, loving head

10

—a large connexion has lost one of its most beloved members—society has lost a man of much usefulness and Christian worth—for myself, I have lost a good counsellor and a faithful and confiding friend ; and you, as a congregation, have lost an office-bearer whose place it will not be easy to supply.

" How often in private have many of you heard his earnest counsels ; at how many sickbeds and deathbeds have you been comforted by his consolations ; how often, here and elsewhere, have we heard his earnest pleading voice in prayer ; and how often has that voice been lifted up in wrestling intercession for us all, when there was no ear to hear but that of our Father in Heaven."

LIFE DECLINING.

It was in April, 1881, that Mr. Black so felt the need of rest that he obtained leave of absence from the Presbytery of Manitoba and went to Ontario and to his old home in New York State, seeking health. After spending some months in the east and being present at the meeting of the General Assembly, he returned to Manitoba, feeling much improved. Unfortunately he caught a severe cold on his return journey and was again reduced in strength. Reaching Kildonan he sought to minister to his devoted people, but after a few Sabbaths was again compelled to make application to the presbytery for relief. This was granted most willingly, but at the same time with a feeling of great anxiety on the part of his brethren. It seemed the presage of the approaching end. The affectionate attention of friends and relations was given him, but he remained very weak. Reclining on his sofa, he received his ministerial and other friends, and still with clear mind discoursed on the topics of the day and on the blessedness of the service of Christ with the great future rewards of the people of God. Even in the time of declining strength his was no weak or halting faith, but a strong and unwavering confidence.

The old year passed away and the opening days of January saw no marked change. His interest in the affairs of the parish did not flag, but he was patiently resigned in his weakening strength. At last as the opening hours of the second Sabbath, 12th, of February, 1882, were approaching, the spirit of the devoted minister passed away to its eternal rest. The event, though somewhat expected, yet produced a shock in the parish, and on the word reaching Winnipeg references were made in the city pulpits on that day to the departure of the good man.

TRIBUTES.

The tributes of kind friends came from all directions. The leading newspaper of the province referred to the great service he had rendered the whole Northwest, and said : "In the midst of his many duties he was able in a wonderful degree to keep abreast of the literature of the day. Although occupying so remote a field, he was remarkable for the superiority of his scholarship, so that he enjoyed an eminent reputation as a man of learning and particularly as a theologian."

LAST SAD RITES.

On the following Wednesday the funeral took place, the service being held in Kildonan church. The day was one of the most bitterly cold days of the season. Yet the people of all denominations were there, and representatives from the river parishes and Winnipeg, so that the church was pretty well filled with men and women.

Several of the oldest members of the presbytery were absent from the province at the time, and were prevented from paying their last tokens of respect to the departed leader. Rev. Professor Hart, who had been for ten years intimately acquainted with Mr. Black, took the service and made the address. In the course of his remarks he said: " In reference to Dr. Black's public life, I have only a word or two to say. As a preacher he was well known to us all as being clear, forcible, simple, impressive and eloquent in his exposition of divine truths; as a pastor he was indefatigable, visiting regularly in succession all the families in his parish, especially in times of sickness, distress or in death. He was active in forwarding the interest of the Sabbath-school and also of the Bible Society, of which for years he was president.

" Every good cause found in him a faithful and zealous advocate. As a friend, the departed was judicious, faithful, steadfast and true. His whole course among us was, I may add, such as became a true and faithful man of God. When work was to be done he did it up to the measure of his strength and even beyond it. Hence, though naturally of a strong and healthy constitution, he succumbed—not to old age, but to excess of work. He was worn out by his exertions, and his death took place at a time when in his prime, intellectually, years of activity and usefulness might be looked forward to.

"The All Wise Disposer of events seemed to say that our friend's work on earth was done, and called for him from labour and trial here to the rest that remains for the just. The last illness of our brother (and father), though protracted to nearly a year, was not during the latter portion of it accompanied with much pain. To the end his faith re-

PUBLIC MONUMENT ERECTED TO REV. JOHN BLACK, D.D.
In Kildonan churchyard.

mained unshaken, his hope undimmed, his peace of mind
undisturbed. That end came quietly. He sweetly fell
asleep in the arms of Jesus. Just as that day he loved the
best was being ushered in, just as that earthly Sabbath
dawned, he passed away to the enjoyment of an eternal
Sabbath in the courts above."

The Rev. Alexander Matheson, a native of Kildonan,
then led in prayer ; the Rev. C. B. Pitblado, the minister of
the new St. Andrew's congregation of Winnipeg, pronounced
the benediction ; the Rev. Alexander Campbell was also
present, and the Rev. R. Y. Thompson took the service at
the grave.

RETROSPECT.

We have now completed our long journey from Garwald-
shields farm in Eskdale Muir, where John Black was born,
to Kildonan kirkyard, where his honoured bones now lie.
Sixty-four years was his alloted span, and no one who has
followed our story can fail to admit that the character and
life described are those of a true man.

Born among the shepherd people of the region that has
been made historic by the names of Thomas Boston, James
Hogg, Edward Irving and Thomas Carlyle, the worthy lad
of Eskdale very early showed the features of a religious
and deep-laid character. What he would have been had
he remained in the land of his birth we can only conjecture,
but it is certain that wherever he was to dwell his earnest,
manly, studious boyhood was the promise of a useful life.

Perhaps nothing shows the chivalry of his nature more
than his surrendering all the bright hopes of a student life,
and the career of a successful teacher, in order that he might
with his family, which had suffered losses, seek a New World
home to better their condition. His unselfish devotion led

to his becoming the mainstay in the counsels of the family as they settled in the State of New York. Years afterwards we find his love of his aged parents in the Catskills a matter for consideration in choosing where his lot should be cast.

The return of John Black to the Canadian branch of the Church of his fathers illustrates two or three points in his character. There was in him a strong attachment to old associations. The Scottish type of Presbyterianism was to him the best, and he sought his defence in the shelter of the "burning bush." His characteristic discrimination and determination to follow his convictions were shown in his choice of the newly formed Free Church, while his love of the past and strong personal attachment would have led him to cling to the Church of Scotland. His love of country was also strong, and there can be no doubt that he greatly preferred the shadow of the Union Jack to that of any other flag.

His student and missionary life were characterized by great thoroughness and enthusiasm. While strongly evangelical, and counting all things other than the Gospel as "wood and hay and stubble," yet he valued knowledge, and laid the foundation of subsequent excellence in Latin, Greek, History, and English Literature. His missionary life in Brock, in Upper Canada, in the district of Montreal, and on behalf of the French Canadian Society, all indicates the spirit of thorough consecration, which is the beauty and strength of the aspirant to the Christian ministry. The most critical time in the life of John Black was his reception of the command, for it was nothing else, of Dr. Burns to go to Red River Settlement. Those who knew Dr. Burns can easily imagine the ardency and enthusiasm with which he would argue the case. He was a man of strong personality, and to him his opinions had all the strength of principles. Mr. Black could not resist what was put to him as the call of duty. It is somewhat remarkable to see, however, that year after year he was not convinced that the Red River was to be his permanent sphere of labor. This no doubt arose from a certain sensitiveness of disposition, and an unwillingness to stand in the way of what he thought was the highest spiritual good of his people. And yet it was as all his friends said it would be : God's finger pointed out the Red River unmistakably as his lifelong sphere.

The founding of a new cause among a people who, for thirty or forty years had been without their own form of faith, was a great work. The church building, the alarming flood which hindered his work, the severe task of supplying, while still alone, the small groups of Presbyterians outside of Kildonan, the anxiety about the spiritual condition and insobriety of so many of the native people about him, cases of discipline which required at the same time firmness and tact—all these filled up the measure of his busy life.

The effect of the arrival of an additional laborer in the person of Rev. James Nisbet, in 1862, can hardly be estimated by us now. The fact that another clergyman may arrive now in the field of Manitoba missions is an everyday occurrence, and gives rise to little comment ; but when the arrival of a laborer doubled the available missionary force it made it an event of first importance. When, four years later, James Nisbet began the Indian missions of the Church it was something, too, of immense moment. John Black's dream of fifteen years was then realized, and he saw in the future the vista of a reclaimed and civilized race in place of the helpless and sin-afflicted savages by whom he was surrounded.

When the stirring days of the Riel Rebellion were over, there came the rush of immigration, which startled the quiet solitudes of the Red River prairies. It was to Mr. Black, as to the older people of the country, a time of change, but the religious needs of the new settlements were well looked after, and the movement begun of the mission advance, which has been so notable a feature of the Presbyterian cause in the Northwest, and has led to the Church, which John Black came to the west to found, becoming much the largest and most influential body of the prairies.

Not only in Winnipeg, with its thoroughly organized body of communicants, and in Portage la Prairie, Brandon, Regina and Calgary have the Presbyterian views of church doctrine and life become potential; but, in more than a score of towns, such as Morden, Pilot Mound, Deloraine, Carman, Glenboro, Treherne, Holland, Miami, Minnedosa, Russell, Rapid City, Gladstone, Moosomin, Prince Albert, Edmonton, Souris, Virden, Boissevain, Emerson, Keewatin, Rat Portage, Fort William, and Port Arthur have strong self-sustaining churches been established. Notably is the Church strongly ensconced in the affections of the agricultural communities spread over the prairies. It would gladden the heart of John Black to-day could he see the presbytery of which he was the first moderator now developed into two synods with fourteen presbyteries, and could he realize how " the little one has become a thousand."

As an educationist, we have shown the really fundamental work of Mr. Black in the cause of education. It is very rare to see the men who lay foundations equally strong on the missionary and on the educational sides. It shows

the even balance of his mind, that Mr. Black was as much
interested in one direction as in the other. Manitoba College is the outcome to-day of the hopes and pleadings and
plans of this scion, transplanted from the parish schools of
Scotland, and of the early love of knowledge of the Presbyterianism of Canada, which took root in the favorable soil
of the Red River, Assiniboine, and Saskatchewan valleys.

These are the memorials of the Apostle of Red River.
We are not carried away by any absurd sentiment which would
lead us to make John Black a hero. As a rule the surroundings of his life were not of an exciting kind. The
Red River community was isolated, its opportunities of
communication with the outer world were small ; for two-
thirds of the life of John Black upon the Red River there
was little increase in the population, but during his thirty
years of Northwest life we see in him the white lily of a
blameless life, we see the spirit of an ardent social reformer,
we see the public sentiment leading him to labor for the
educational good of his people, we see the exercise of a dil-
igent pastorate, and the attainment of honorable distinction as a preacher—in short, we see in him the embodiment of high domestic, social, public and Christian virtues.
We shall cherish the memory of " the Apostle of the Red
River."